THE HOWLING OF SATAN'S TEMPLE

and other tales

H. R. Brown

ISBN-13: 979-8451318492

For Barbara & Ralph, George & Vicky,
for everything.

CONTENTS

ACKNOWLEDGMENTS

Creative facilitation for the cover image was provided by
Rowena La Thor
(roboots337@yahoo.co.uk).

Other acknowledgments include; the internet, pop culture
and pop music.

THE HOWLING OF SATAN'S TEMPLE

It was the howling that did it. Tore through everything. I see that now. No man wants to hear his mother and his great-auntie, howling like that. Clinging to each other in the street outside the bar, sobbing and raging at the sky. It's as if howling breeds itself.

Yet what were they to do? Fiona was dead. There was no recourse. My second cousin Fiona was signed into the bar when it happened, and had not signed out. The police had confirmed; death by molten magma, in licensed premises, victim present at own risk. Case closed.

There were commiserations from various folk who'd left the bar after it happened, but I had to shoo them off. I stood guard for some time. The ladies were in no mood to speak to anyone, including me.

Later, when my toes and mind were numb with it all, and mum and great-aunt Dottie could now only whimper with hopeless regret and bury their faces in each others arms, it was time to go. The policeman, who had also remained behind, motioned to me. We lifted them into his carriage. The horses trotted swiftly through the night and we were back on our street within half an hour.

I didn't sleep.

I'd seen it before, of course. Occasional bar room brawls
end that way, as they have since the Great Accord, nearly
three hundred years ago. Some drunken brawls take more
than just one pisshead on power-poach to quell the discord.
My brother was present at the worst one in the vale this
century - when four young men went out in one almighty
fight. Two brothers each, from two clans. The third and
final brother of each clan fought tooth and nail for fully
fifteen minutes, before Peterson fell to Wolstenholme's final
blow.

Wolstenholme heaved the beaten Peterson aloft and prepared
to hurl him into the nearest lava pit, when Sadie Peterson
stopped him. She pledged herself there and then, in clear
sight of the bar staff and remaining spectators, to be
Wolstenholme's wife forever, if he would spare her brother's
life. He hadn't trusted her until she pointed out that the
within these walls she took the oath, in sight of qualified bar
staff, and within these walls she would willingly stand to
face her judgement if she lied. "Please," she had begged
him, "Both our mothers will suffer for this day to the end of
their lives. Let both keep a son, and I will give yours a
daughter."

It was the stuff of legend. Tragic, horrifying, majestic,
legend.

Just once, I'd watched the whole process happen. Very early
on in my pub-going life, I'd spent the night in a bar, aged
only sixteen (two years early in legal terms, obviously,
though history tells us it's the average age for us Brits). The

guy who was thrown over the edge was a friend of the two who threw him in, but he was the runt of the litter. The other two had grown tired of him. I raced over to the well to watch the never-won fight of man vs magma. The screaming, slowly-sinking man as he writhed around, maniacally, formed a pattern of horror unique to such victims. The other two molten deaths I've witnessed confirm this. A human will sink quite slowly into lava; burning and boiling simultaneously, a frenzy of thrashing, clawing wildly - yet hopelessly - up at the walls of the well and those watching from above, eyes popping with horror and agony, inch by appalling inch, shrieking like nothing you ever want to hear again. Shrieking that can't be replicated by any other means; lungs both screaming and boiling make that very clear.

The second time I couldn't watch, but I saw the man get thrown in and I heard him. It took some time.

I'd seen it before, of course - but never this close to home. And this, *this* was my third. And I saw it. How could I not? I was completely mortified when I saw her get knocked over the edge - instinct took over and I ran to try to help. But of course there is no help for anyone who goes in. That's it. Every lava well is seven feet in diameter, walled all round by just three and a half feet of stone wall. If you go over the edge and don't manage to grab hold of it - it's a twelve foot drop directly into Hell. And I saw Fiona in hell. Writhing, howling, begging and I was screaming and someone was pulling me back and I got dragged away by two or three blokes but I could still hear her. I always will.

I spent that night oscillating between despondency and rage.

What kind of civilisation are we? What ever was wrong with the ancients' way of drinking, in pubs not built upon pits of molten lava? I cursed the Petrovitch Drilling Method which had allowed humanity to tap safely and easily through the earth's crust for a new source of power. I cursed Muslims and Christians both alike; that their bitter, two-hundred year war had finally been settled by allowing alcohol to all - but only under these ridiculous, barbaric conditions. All booze has to be drunk in licensed bars or 'Temples' (as they were so magnificently decreed) - or it's the rest of your life doing hard labour. I cursed we British, so dependant on booze that our (allegedly) once-great nation had given in and had – under the pitiful banner of 'Our Proud Viking Heritage' – learned to live under the rules of the Great Accord.

Finally, and whole-hollow-heartedly, I cursed myself, so well-weaned on this nature that I knew, even this very same night, that I would not forsake my visits to Satan's Temple.

But I saved my worst venom for Derek Steven McTariff. The man who knocked her in. It was a crappy bar fight. No-one involved looked angry enough for it to end in a toasting. Fiona was unlucky, they said. It was a terrible accident, they said. Wrong place, wrong time, they said. It's a crying shame, they told me, tearlessly.

To give Derek Steven McTariff his due, he did look mortified afterwards. Howled his apologies to all and sundry and fled in fear of his life. And so he should. He should have kept running and he should never have looked back. For I knew the secret which, it later turned out, no-one else knew. I alone saw the disturbing nature of the beast.

Fiona had confided in me, two days prior to her death, of Derek Steven McTariff's shoddy advances to her, and how she had had to gently spurn them because she already had a fella.

I was howling in the darkness. DSM would pay, and pay dearly.

Fiona's bloke, Jim Saunders was all but destroyed by her death. He wasn't the violent type, and had accepted that DSM had not meant to kill anyone. I managed to get Jim to come with me for a drink, two weeks later. My rage had settled now into a hardened knot. I wanted an explosion. I talked quietly and firmly. I explained everything I knew, very carefully. Jim went from being a broken man to being a very angry man. When I had finished, he necked the rest of his beer, practically tore our table from its housing, rushed to the bar and laid the foundations for a magnificent hangover. He demanded I match him, shot for shot, while he quizzed me further and further on what I knew. I didn't disappoint him.

Before long, Jim Saunders was frothing with fury and swearing death to Derek Steven McTariff. And then, as if on cue, DSM appeared with two of his friends.

Jim was silent. He stared at DSM and calmly knocked back two more shots of tequila and washed them down with more than half a pint of lager. I said nothing, just tried to keep up.

Jim stood up. He walked over to DSM, who was a slightly larger man than him, and asked him directly;

"Did you try to get off with Fiona, the week you killed her?"

The rest of the pub fell silent. DSM was horrified. I could see in his eyes the very thing that had slithered into my veins and I knew it then beyond doubt.

Derek Steven McTariff looked at his two mates for support, yet they were now looking askance at him, waiting for an answer. DSM looked back at Jim, who stood absolutely still and intent. He couldn't hide the blush, and when he said -

"No! No I didn't!"

- it was a palpable lie. I have never seen a man go as ape-shit as Jim went that moment. Fists were frenzied, DSM was staggered and then Jim threw him into the nearest pit. This time the sound was music to me, and I went over to the well to watch his every last wretched spasm.

I watched for at least two minutes. It felt like a penance and a blessing and a tithe. Afterwards I would remember to my alarm that I didn't flinch at, or even heed the stench of the steam as it billowed around me.

But I hadn't reckoned with Davy McTariff, come to join his brother and their friends for a drink. He howled like nothing I had ever heard when he realised, and Jim, bowed again by the weight of his thoughts, didn't realise until Davy was already pounding him in the face.

Now I came to life and tried to hold Davy back, tried to tell him what his brother had done but he knocked me to the ground like a man possessed. He tore into Jim and threw him into another lava well. That awful noise began again.

I staggered outside and I howled my guilt at the silver

summer moon. I threw up and I howled even more. And here I am, howling my soul at the sky. It was the howling that did it. Tore through everything.

PERCEPTECH

Friday night, and Larry Quince was late getting home. Whilst on the bus he planned all the things he was going to do to make good on his lost time. He had already been to the bank for funds, so that was sorted. First thing; sweep Janet onto the couch and give her a damn good reminder that he loved her. Second; call the dealer to arrange for a bag of the good stuff - they were almost out. While waiting for the guy, they would call their various friends, knock up a quick meal, eat, and then get ready for the pub. As soon as the dealer got there, they would pay him, stash the gear safely and head off out.

When he got through the door, she was waiting for him with a rolling pin in her hands.

"Where the hell have you been?" she asked, seeming impassive.

"Sorry," he said, "Couldn't help it. Johnson kept me late to finish some *ever-so-vital* file management, then the bus was late. How are you?"

"The landlord just called round," she told him, her voice still neutral, "And he wants to know why this month's cheque bounced."

Larry was taken aback. "It can't have," he said, "I checked the balance the other day, I know how much I've taken out tonight - we should still have the rent plus twenty. When did you last use it?"

"Don't you give me that!" she cried, "I went to the bank to check - here!"

She passed him a statement and prodded her finger at it.

"What the hell is *this*?!"

Larry followed her finger to the debit of fifty quid, logged five days since. It was an online transaction. He frowned. "I've no idea!" he said, "That's gotta be wrong!"

Janet's pretty face took on that dangerous look of absolute certainty which he knew rather too well. "Well I know one thing for goddamn sure - it was not me. Look at the time on it!"

It was not only an online transaction which he was sure he had not made, but it was logged at 4:13am.

"Hang on," he said,

"NO!" Janet screamed at him, "I won't 'hang on'! You've always been irresponsible, I know that, but paying fifty quid online to the Perceptech Corporation at four in the morning - do you think I can't guess what you were up to!?"

"What do you mean?" said Larry, flabbergasted.

"I've heard about Perceptech moving into porn!" Janet snarled, raising the rolling pin, "I know exactly what you were doing!"

"Wait," he said, "Last Saturday night we got to bed after two on Sunday morning - don't you remember?"

Janet held back the rolling pin for a moment, considering.

"We were at Jeb's party 'till at least half one," he said, urgently, pressing his advantage, "And when we got back I would have passed out fully clothed on the bed, except you managed to keep me awake for maybe half an hour or so - don't you remember?" he smiled, knowing she hadn't forgotten their haphazard, drunken romp.

Janet was looking confused. "That was last Sunday, early in the morning?"

"You know it was! You know the party was on Saturday night - check your calendar! And after we'd finished, well, we both just passed out didn't we? We must have been completely gone by three a.m. And you're suggesting I got up one hour later and went on the internet? This is bollocks! We've been *robbed*!"

Janet lowered the rolling pin. "Shit," she said, "You're right! You passed out before me! What are we going to do?"

"I'll call the landlord. I get paid soon enough - we can sort out two rent payments for him, no problem, but we'll have to be a bit careful next month. And I'll get in touch with these cheeky mothers and get our money back."

"It's Friday night!" Janet moaned, "This is *shit*!"

"Yeah, I was about to call the dealer as well!"

"Oh, we'll deal with it tomorrow. Let's just go to the pub and forget it!"

Larry remembered his plans. "First thing's first," he told her, taking her in his arms.

"Oh yeah?" she said, wide eyed, "What *did* you have in mind!?"

***

Their local was buzzing with friendly faces and good-natured, yet salacious, gossip; with loud, drunken roars of appreciation, the crack of pool balls and with couples being overly friendly. It was a good night, enjoyed by all.

The next day Larry and Janet arose late and had bacon butties with coffee for breakfast, followed by more coffee and a shared spliff.

"Right," said Larry, lazily, "I'm calling 'em."

"Who?"

"Perceptech!"

"Go for it!"

The automated female voice on the other end of the line gave Larry a hard time. Eventually, after five minutes of pressing the required buttons to let him through the proper gaps in the call-screening process, Larry was put on hold for an actual operator.

Five minutes after that, a male, human, voice - which managed to sound infinitely more dull and lifeless than the automaton had been - said,

"Hello, Perceptech, Michael speaking, how can I help you?"

"Hello Michael!" said Larry, "You can help me by telling me why it is that I've been charged fifty quid for an online transaction which I know I've not made."

"OK sir," the voice droned, in terminal boredom, "Could you give me your name, time of transaction and reference number, please."

These were all on the bank statement, and Larry read them out accordingly.

There was a pause.

"Hello?" said Larry, "*Hello*!?"

"I'm sorry Mr Quince," said the operative, "The transaction was carried out as per our obligations and we are under no legal obligation to reimburse you."

"What!? What the hell are you talking about!? I was asleep at the time - I never bought a damn thing!"

"I'm sorry sir," the voice continued with the same, indefatigable monotone, "We have all the necessary proofs and documentation upon the sale - these will be with you shortly."

"WHAT GODDAMN SALE!?!" Larry roared, "I was asleep at four-bloody-thirteen that morning; do you understand me?

I was never online and I never made any, goddamn transaction!"

"If you'd be good enough to wait for the package which will be with you by this time next week sir," the voice continued, vacuously, "You will receive answers to all your queries. Goodbye."

"What!? WAIT! I want a decent explanation as to what it is that I'm supposed to have bought and who gave you permission to debit our account!"

But the line was dead.

"You could have tried not swearing at him," Janet reproached him, mildly.

This brought yet more colourful descriptions of Larry's utter annoyance, before he settled slightly and said,

"What are we going to do - sue the Perceptech Corporation? Pah! We'd have more luck suing Donald's Muck."

He breathed out slowly in defeat.

"I'm sure there are watchdogs we can tell about this," said Janet.

"No, the bloke told me that, whatever it is, it'll be here soon. We can just send it back and get our money back that way."

"Oh, OK. Let's roll another!"

"Or even - let's have another roll!"

"Even better!"

***

The following Friday night, Larry had practically forgotten about the missing fifty quid, but when he got through the door the look on Janet's face and the rolling pin in her hands brought him an eerie sense of deja-vu which made him instantly think of the previous Friday.

"What?" he asked, nervously.

Janet said nothing. She beckoned him into the living room, where she sat him down on the sofa, turned on the TV and the DVD player.

"What is it?" he persisted, but Janet remained mute and played the DVD.

The logo flashed up on the screen:

PERCEPTECH

- followed by a few other brief logos along the lines of 'in association with'.

Then a man appeared who looked and spoke like a US news presenter.

"Hello, good citizen," the man said, "And congratulations on buying your first inter-erotic DVD - eroticism for the future. On behalf of the Perceptech Corporation, we thank you and hope this disc gives you everything you asked for - and more!"

Larry was watching with increasing anger. "I didn't bloody *ask* for anything!" he shouted.

"Shhh," Janet said, "Watch."

The screen grew vivid with the words:

INTEROTIC DVD

PRESENTS:

which was followed by;

LARRY QUINCE

DISC 1

"What the...?" said Larry.

The screen went completely black, then slowly it began to brighten into a strange seascape. The beach was bright, golden yellow, the sea a gorgeous, Mediterranean blue and the sky an unusual shade of pink. Larry sat bolt upright. He had seen this somewhere before...

"Recognise it?" Janet asked.

"Well, yeah, but I don't remember where from!"

"Neither did I," she said, quietly, "But I worked it out. Jeb's got a painting of it at his house. It's surrealist, or something."

Larry became even more confused as he saw himself walk into the picture, wearing shorts and a T-shirt which he recognised as his, and wandering contentedly across the sand. The sense of deja-vu was becoming ever more acute, and he found himself beginning to sweat, yet still didn't understand why.

Then he saw Jeb and Lucile having a meal together at their dining table, which was sitting on the beach as if it belonged there. His alter ego on the screen waved and shouted hello to them as he walked past, and they waved back.

Larry felt the warm prickling sensation up the back of his neck. This was familiar in a weird way that made no sense at all. Whatever was about to happen was not going to be pleasant - he knew it, yet knew not what it was.

Then she appeared. The beautiful blonde girl of fantastic proportions, wearing nothing but a tiny pair of denim hot-pants and a white shirt through which her bronzed nipples were obvious.

"Oh, shit!" said Larry out loud, whilst his screen-self seemed oblivious to the woman.

"Hey!" she called out, "Can you help me?"

His screen-self noticed her and seemed impressed. He answered in the affirmative and followed her into a small beach house. Before many more seconds had passed, she was completely naked, and Larry was having a hard time not ogling her in the same way his screen-self was.

"This is bullshit!" he said, "I've never seen this woman in

my life!"

His screen-self remembered something. "Sorry," he said, "I've got a girlfriend."

The blonde laughed a delightful little laugh and said, "Don't worry! Look - look out of the window."

Outside the window, a squadron of pigs zoomed overhead in V-formation. The deafening roar which they produced shook the whole picture.

"See, you big silly!" said the blonde, "This is a dream! You can't be blamed for *dreaming* you're having sex with me, can you? It's not like you're *really* cheating!"

Larry felt the colour drain from his face. He had just remembered what happened next.

"See," the blonde was telling his screen-self, "Just type in your account number and sort code on this keypad, see, and then, *then*, you can do whatever you want to me. And you'll get a DVD of it, too!"

As his screen-self was eagerly typing in the combination, Larry tried to stand up.

"Ring any bells?" Janet enquired.

"This is bullshit!" he said, walking away from what he knew was coming next on the TV, "This is *absolute* bullshit! I was asleep! How can this be possible? How can it be *legal*!?"

"The legal stuff is all in here," Janet said, passing him a

leaflet bearing the Perceptech logo. "Sit down, you're missing it."

Larry, fuming and sick to his stomach, turned back to the TV to see his screen/dream-self performing oral sex on the beautiful, naked blonde.

"We haven't got to the good bit yet!" Janet told him, "I never realised that men really do have bigger dicks in their dreams!"

Larry couldn't watch any more. "How can this be possible?" he muttered.

"THAT'S JUST WHAT I WANT TO KNOW!" screamed Janet, and the next thing Larry knew, she was beating him around his shoulders and his back with the rolling pin.

Enraged with the entire situation, Larry tried to fend off her attacks without hitting her back, but she was like an animal, continually giving him the slip and whacking him some more. Eventually, after she had caught him flagging, and weakened with a couple of good whacks, Larry forgot himself, forgot the pain and grabbed her savagely, forcing her down onto the floor and, falling on top of her, he pinned her down by both arms.

Caught here on the floor, facing each other, panting and growling, Larry remembered himself and loosened his grip slightly. Janet, for her part, gave a little giggle, and said,

"Gonna have me then, or what!?"

BURGLAR ALARM

Dermott McKeever whistled along to the power-guitar rock music that was booming out of the mega megawatt speakers of his car's hi-fi system. It was a fine day, and he was feeling fantastic. He was sure that his bid for financing from the **PERCEPTECH** Corporation was about to be approved. The first real test of the new system he'd been working on looked like being a great success. In all honesty, it couldn't fail. It was the perfect instrument.

His big car glided smoothly up the road, round a corner and smashed straight into three small children who were running hell for leather down the hill, in the middle of the road.

The tyres felt like they were part of his own body as they screeched and tore at the road to cease motion. The car and its driver stayed totally still for a minute or two. His body, taut like industrial cable, gripped the wheel and pushed against the seatbelt until he could feel it beginning to cut the skin under his shirt. They hadn't moved yet. He could see them in his mirrors, and the only thing he was certain of was the gathering pools of blood around each of their spread-eagled, broken, little bodies.

In time he made himself leave the car, and call 999. For a minute he flew into a rage, he charged from one prostrate child to another, screaming at them and cursing and begging *why*? Why the middle of the road, had their parents taught them nothing?! It was almost as if they had been fleeing from something terrible... Then McKeever remembered where he had been going and for what reason.

He sat down quietly in the middle of the road.

***

Timmy Willis wandered carefree down the road. It was Saturday, the sun was shining and the half-term holiday was just starting.

He met Spence at the usual place and the two of them went to the park.

"Jim got beat up last night," said Spence, swinging his legs back and forth.

"What for?"

"Whaddya mean, 'what for'?! He's Jim, in't he? He were reading a book on the school bus!"

Timmy laughed. He reached out, testing the strength of the next branch up.

"He's clever, is Jim," he said, "But there's some stuff he never learns."

"Did'ja see that fire last night?" asked Spence.

Timmy's new branch wobbled, dangerously, so he let it be.

"What fire?" he said, annoyed, searching for another option.

"That new house, up Daisy Bank," said Spence, "Part of it were on fire last night!"

"Yeah?"

"Yeah, and I tell you sommat else, an all - there were no fire engines turned up."

"No? Did it burn right down?"

"Don't think so. Fire just seemed to go out, after a bit. D'you wanna go have a look?"

"Why?"

Spence tutted. "It were on *fire*!" he said.

Timmy realised he wasn't going to be able to climb any higher. Was it worth trying the next tree?

"A'right," he said, then he swung down from the branch he had been standing on and leapt out of the tree.

Spence hesitated, then awkwardly followed suit. He landed rather badly and hurt his ankle. Timmy had to stifle his laughter when he saw that his friend was near tears.

"You OK?" he said, helping Spence up.

"I'll be right," said Spence.

They walked up the hill together, with Spence complaining and Timmy finding it funnier and funnier, though he didn't laugh. On the way, they met Stella Douthwaite.

"What you two doing?" she wanted to know.

"Minding our own business," said Spence.

Stella rolled her pretty eyes. "I dunno what you two see in each other!" she said, maliciously.

"Fuck off!" said Timmy.

"No!" said Stella, "Think I wanna walk up Daisy Bank an all."

The boys stopped and looked at each other.

"Oh God!" said Spence, "A'right then, but keep yer gob shut."

They carried on walking.

"Where you going?" Stella asked.

"Thought I said keep yer gob shut!" yelled Spence.

"Gonna make me?"

"There were a fire up here last night," said Timmy.

"Oh, nice one Tim!" said Spence in disgust.

"Up at that new house?" said Stella, "I saw that!"

"Yeah?" said Timmy.

The two of them started talking, and Spence said not one more word until they got there.

The house was some way off the main road, in a plot all of its own. It was a big, smart, white house with a black-slate roof and it was completely surrounded by small, newly-planted evergreen trees.

Nothing stirred except for the three youngsters, moving cautiously up the driveway. They got to the house to find it looking pristine and unblemished.

"There were definitely a fire here!" Stella piped up, and the boys hushed her, furiously.

They circled round the building, looking in through the big, double-glazed windows. The house was sparsely-decorated and mostly empty, though they could see that one room alone contained a TV, a computer and peripherals, DVD player, camcorder, micro-jukebox linked to multiple speakers and a huge library of CDs, vinyls and DVDs.

"Somebody's been shopping," Spence whispered.

Having gone all the way around the building, they could find no sign of any fire.

Spence was frowning. "It were right here!" he hissed, pointing at the windows of the spacious, ultra modern kitchen.

"Yeah," said Stella, "This were it!"

The kitchen was a bright, purpose-built unit. There were all kinds of flowers sitting in the window boxes.

"Are those flowers flame-proof?" said Timmy.

"They could be," said Spence, "They might be lined with asbestos or sommat."

"This is bollocks," said Timmy, "There's not been any fires here. I bet you can't even see this house from yours - there's too many trees in the way!"

"Then how come I can see my house from here?" asked Stella.

"Bollocks," said Timmy.

"Oh, we'll see," said Stella, and she marched up to the front door and rang the bell.

"Shit," said Spence, "What's she doing now?"

Stella waited, and waited. She rang again. No answer. She rang for longer, and waited again. The boys joined her at the door.

"No-one in," she said.

Spence tried the handle, and the door opened. The three of them looked at each other in astonished glee. No-one said anything. They all went in.

They soon found the TV room, and began checking out the contents of the video and audio libraries.

"Look at all these CDs!" said Stella, "Afrodiva, The Cool Hand Gang, Bra Wars, Will Robbins, Then 42, Red Keith, Knickerless,... It's like they've been and got all the top albums this week!"

"Look at these DVDs," Spence crowed, "They've got Triple Z, Golden Bazooker, Captain Selfless,... Oh!" His eyes were wide with his next discovery - "And they've got Bloodzest

III: The Zombie Rape Machine! God, my mum wouldn't get me this for Christmas!"

He picked up the DVD box, then frowned. He suddenly felt very queasy. He held his mouth, instinctively and looked at his friends. Timmy and Stella were both caught in a moment of panic, holding their own mouths.

Spence was the first to pop. He threw up hugely; the pink, acidic goo with carrots and onions poured out of him, burning his throat and doubling him over. The sight, smell and sound of it was enough to send Timmy and Stella over the edge as well.

The vomit was everywhere, and the three children had sunk to their knees with their horrible efforts. They sat there, gasping and crying for a few seconds, before the vomit arose from the floor.

Timmy screamed, as the horrendous, slimy beast swiped Stella's head clean off. The blood exploded up out of her severed neck, and splashed all over Spence, who was immobile and white with shock. The beast split him in two, lengthways.

The room, so clean only moments ago, was awash with fresh humanity.

Timmy was at the door, still screaming. He had opened it to find an invisible force like a steel wall across the door-frame, preventing him leaving the room. In terror, he turned around, and saw the floor rush up to bang his forehead. The room spun, and through the agony and the blood, he saw his own headless corpse collapse down on top of him, then nothing more.

***

"Look at all these CDs!" said Stella, "Afrodiva, The Cool Hand Gang, Bra Wars, Will Robbins, Then 42, Red Keith, Knickerless,... It's like they've been and got all the top albums this week!"

Then they all stopped and looked at each other, wildly.

"What the fuck is going on?" Timmy spluttered.

"Did that *happen*?" said Stella.

"Fucking-well felt real enough for me!" Spence cried, "I'm gettin' out!"

He raced out of the door, followed by Timmy.

Stella grabbed the Knickerless CD and ran after them to find they were lying in the hall, slowly melting onto the carpet, like candle wax. Then the pain hit her, and she too fell to the floor. She writhed around in agony, unable to scream, while her flesh bubbled and slowly trickled off her body. Her last vision was that of Spence's eyeballs draining down the cheekbone of his skull.

***

"Look at all these CDs!" said Stella, "Afrodiva, The Cool Hand Gang, Bra Wars, Will Robbins, Then 42, Red Keith, Knickerless,... It's like they've been and got all the top albums this week!"

Then they all stopped and looked at each other, wildly.

"We can't get out!" said Spence, starting to cry, "We can't get out before it starts! It's gonna get us again and again and again and we can't stop it!" he was sobbing, "*What we gonna do*!?"

Timmy was mute though his eyes moved dementedly, fearing everything, looking for a quicker way out.

"I think it might be my fault," said Stella, with tears in her eyes, "I took a CD, last time."

"You did what?!" cried Spence, the tears all down his cheeks, "You stupid fucking cow!" he screamed at her, "*You stupid fucking cow!*"

He leapt at her throat and the two of them crashed into a glass table, with Stella sobbing the words, "I'm sorry!" and "Stop it, please!" and suddenly the room was exploding and machine-gun fire was ripping into all of them.

As he lay dying through no fault of his own, Timmy thought desperately about what to do - would there be a way out? He could feel his life slipping away, and despite what had happened, every instinct told him to fight, to struggle, to do anything not to give in and die, because how could he be certain that this *wouldn't* be the end?

It was happening every time they touched something they shouldn't, and that meant that, meant that, there was something, but what was it again?

***

"Look at all these CDs!" said Stella, "Afrodiva, The Cool Hand Gang, Bra Wars, Will Robbins, Then 42, Red Keith, Knickerless,... It's like they've been and got all the top albums this week!"

Then they all stopped and looked at each other, wildly.

"*You fucking twat*!" Stella screamed at Spence, "Whose fucking fault were it that time?"

She leapt at him, screaming, "*Fucking bastard*!"

"Stop it, for fuck's sake!" Timmy shouted, but too late. In their fighting, they knocked into the TV.

The floor rumbled, then gave way. Screaming, the children fell headfirst into the black abyss.

The acceleration of an object in free fall is a slave to gravity, and gravity has no mercy. The children soon knew they would not survive the fall. What they couldn't see, in the utter darkness, was the enormous, jagged, steel blades waiting for them a quarter of a mile below, set into stone and pointing directly upwards.

***

"Look at all these CDs!" said Stella, "Afrodiva, The Cool Hand Gang, Bra Wars, Will Robbins, Then 42, Red Keith, Knickerless,... It's like they've been and got all the top albums this week!"

Then they all stopped and looked at each other, wildly.

Timmy burst away, through the door, through the hall and

out! He was out of the house! But he wasn't going to trust it, not yet. He didn't stop, or even slow down as he raced down the driveway as fast as he was able.

It wasn't long before he heard a sickeningly-loud, booming, crash from behind him. Then he did stop, and he looked back at the house to see it disintegrating into a molten inferno.

***

"Look at all these CDs!" said Stella, "Afrodiva, The Cool Hand Gang, Bra Wars, Will Robbins, Then 42, Red Keith, Knickerless,... It's like they've been and got all the top albums this week!"

Then they all stopped and looked at each other, wildly.

"No!" cried Timmy, "NOOOOOOOOO!" he screamed, "NOOOOOOOOO! I can't get away and there's no stopping it and you two - you keep fucking killing me!"

Stella was still too mortified by her previous burning alive, to even register the two boys anymore. The chill set in her veins, and words no longer had meaning. Each sickening death was worse than the last, and burning to death was one of her most horrifying fears. She looked on with dull eyes whilst Timmy started a fight with Spence. She already knew she was doomed again, but she began to see the cold beauty of it. This time, the earth began to move, more and more, harder and harder, and the house collapsed in upon them under the structural duress of the tremors.

And now the nightmare took on a far more vicious

dimension. None of the children died straightaway. They lay buried alive under the rubble of the house for hours. They called out to each other, to their parents - in vain. They drifted in and out of consciousness, and their internal injuries slowly killed them.

***

"Look at all these CDs!" said Stella, "Afrodiva, The Cool Hand Gang, Bra Wars, Will Robbins, Then 42, Red Keith, Knickerless,... It's like they've been and got all the top albums this week!"

Then they all stopped and looked at each other. Despondency weighed in.

"Please," said Timmy, "No-one move. I think I've got it worked out - it's a defensive thing, like a burglar alarm. All we have to do is not touch anything or break anything, and all of us just get the fuck out - right now!"

"Can't hurt to try," Spence mumbled, though he was past caring.

"Right," said Timmy, "So let's go - COME ON!"

They tip-toed quickly to the door, then turned to see that Stella hadn't moved.

"*Come on!*" they both hissed at her.

She didn't move.

"Oh, great!" Spence said, and he giggled. "She's gone totally bonkers. We're dead. We're all dead!"

"So do me one last favour," Timmy hissed, "Shut the fuck up!"

He ran over to Stella, and grabbed her by the arm. "Come on," he said, "We're going now, and everything's going to be fine, come on."

Thank God, he thought, as Stella passively allowed herself to be led out of the room.

They got to the front door and all piled through, hurriedly.

"We're out!" crowed Spence, "We're fucking OUT! YEEEEEEESSSS!!!"

"Shut the fuck up!" Timmy hissed, "That dunt mean we've got away yet!"

He hurried off, still pulling Stella along.

"Dunnit?" said Spence, paling. He bolted after Timmy and all three children sprinted down the hill, praying that this time they would escape.

Modern Art

The old, battered van pulled up behind the 'Class Act Hotel' in London at 9:30pm. In the darkness, the van had found a shadowy spot amongst the occasional light cast by the infrequently placed street lamps.

Three young men quickly climbed out of the back of the van, all of them in dinner dress. Their black trousers, jackets and bow-ties were in pristine condition, as were their whiter-than-white shirts and their shiny black shoes.

Once out, they all checked their button video cameras and microphones which each man had secreted about his chest. Each got the all-clear from the base, via the mini-speaker in his ear. One of them nipped around to whisper a few rapid words to the driver, and then the van drove off.

Rob looked at Matt. Matt looked at Hazza. Hazza looked at Rob. At exactly the same moment, each man began speaking.

"We gonna do it then, or what?", said Rob.

"We ready, then?", said Hazza.
"Come on ladies, let's go!", said Matt.

There was a general laugh, speedily hushed, then they all

walked across the alleyway to the large, silent back door of the Class Act Hotel building.

"What's the time?", asked Hazza.

"Just gone nine-thirty," said Matt, looking at his wristwatch.

Rob nodded, then did a quick double-knock on the door. He left a slight pause and then knocked once, followed by another pause, then a final double-knock.

The door was opened, and the three, smartly-dressed men went in.

"We really appreciate this Joe!", said Hazza to the chef who had opened the door to them.

"No problem," said Joe, "Just remember; I'm nothing to do with you lot now - and I'll pretend not to know you if I need to."

"That's OK Joe," Rob said, quietly, "You're not on the same course as us anyway - and we aren't going say a thing. Which way is it?"

"Out of this storeroom, straight through the kitchen, through the double doors at the other end."

"Cheers mate!", said Matt.

Matt led Hazza and Rob swiftly out into the kitchen. All three walked quickly and confidently, past the rows of silver ovens, the trolleys and the many kitchen staff, some of whom noticed them with an odd look, but said nothing.

One large, middle-aged man - obviously the head chef - stood in their way.

"Where did you lot come from?", he enquired.

Matt and Rob dodged around him without saying a thing, and Hazza stopped in front of him. He took the older man's hand, pressing a fifty-pound note into it, and said,

"Sorry, we're really late, I know! We'll get straight out of your way."

The big head chef looked bemused, but Hazza was off again. He caught up with Rob and Matt, just shy of the double doors.

"Nice one Hazza!", said Matt.

"Yeah, I wasn't actually sure you meant it!", said Rob.

"Don't thank me," said Hazza, "Thank my parents."

"OK, this is it," said Matt.

They walked swiftly through the double doors and out into a vast, plush ball room. The floor was decorated wall-to-wall in an intricate marble pattern of blacks, whites and greys. The high, ornate ceiling was done out in golds and silvers, with huge, diamond chandeliers. The wall on their left had a series of enormous, stained-glass windows, depicting all manner of Biblical fables. The wall on their right was hidden in shadows behind a line of great pillars, expertly carved. The wall behind them was lined with enormous posters for the Annual General Meeting of the Pro-Life

Brigade. The stage ahead of them was decorated in a similar fashion, and colourful bunting flew all around the room.

The scores of tables in the room were separated into two main bodies, with a walkway down the middle and one on either side. The tables were all populated by men dressed as they were, and women wearing all manner of luxurious dresses, which came in every colour of the spectrum. There was a general hum of happy, tipsy banter. Every table had the remnants of many expensive dinners upon it, as well as several bottles of wine. Here and there scurried a servant, generally of a foreign extraction.

The speaker on stage was a big woman of perhaps forty-five to fifty years of age. Her hat was a wicker arrangement, containing a collection of replica exotic fruits. Her dress was equally fruity, being a clever pattern of cherries, berries and other fruits of the forest. She wore many beaded necklaces, rings and her fading blonde hair curled out sideways from underneath the extraordinary headgear she was wearing.

The three newcomers could see that she was coming to the end of her address. Their timing was perfect. She was clearly the illustrious Mrs Pratchett-Gore - the final speaker.

Hazza began skirting round the tables to the left, while Rob and Matt took the right. As they reached their respective back corners of the room, Rob and Matt and Hazza all began heading up the side aisles towards the stage. Halfway up these aisles, they stopped.

Hazza and Rob then stood facing each other, across the

middle of the room. Their button cameras were in perfect placement. Matt kept his eyes on the speaker.

"But we are on our way, dear brothers and sisters," the fruit basket on the stage was saying, "Our rallies have prevented an estimated three-hundred abortions this month alone!"

There was a great cheer from the crowd.

"I know, I know," the smiling speaker said, "We have saved three hundred lives, we have given them all the hope of a bright and full future!"

Matt began to idle his way towards the stage, leaving Rob standing where he was, facing Hazza.

"We are the saviours!", the florally super-adequate Mrs Pratchett-Gore was busy proclaiming, "They may say that any woman should be allowed to choose her own future, they may say that we want to denigrate women, but they can never silence the truth!"

More cheering...

"For we know the truth," she cried, while Matt had almost reached the right-hand stage entry, "We know that any taking of life is always *wrong*! The words 'Thou shalt not kill', are continually used by cowardly politicians to maintain the absence of capital punishment from our justice system, yet who stands up for the innocent babies who are slaughtered in their thousands? The message is getting through, my friends. More and more people are realising that abortion is murder. The numbers committed are shrinking and our lobbyists are reporting significant political gains at Westminster."

Cheers, whoops.

"My friends," she continued, "We will do it. *The end is in sight*!"

People were getting to their feet now, clapping and bawling out their enthusiasm.

Mrs Pratchett-Gore bowed low to her standing ovation. It continued for many a long moment, before she thanked her revolutionary brothers and sisters. "Thank you!", she said, "Thank you all! We shall overcome!"

On and on the shouting and cheering went, as she thanked her audience once more, bowed again, then left the stage.

Matt took a deep breath, then nimbly leapt onto the right-hand end of the stage. He strolled purposefully to the recently-vacated microphone, and took hold of it.

"Ladies and Gentlemen," he announced, a little uncertainly, "I have a special announcement!"

Face forward, he told himself, don't turn too much in either direction, we want a good, six-line realisation...

The crowd's celebratory roaring subsided.

"My friends," Matt began, with increasing confidence, "I have wonderful news!"

He had their attention.

"I'm sorry," he said, "I should introduce myself. My name is Luke Anderson, and I've recently joined our legal department at Docklands. I just want to say that I've been a Pro-lifer since the age of four - when my parents couldn't afford to keep the life which could have become my brother or sister. I'll never know which..."

There was a sudden applause as Matt trailed off, looking suddenly choked. He shook his head slightly and looked up, smiling through the tears. The applause grew.

"I'm sorry," he said, at which the applause grew even louder.

Matt gathered himself ever so well, as they settled down.

"My boss regrets that he was unable to come here himself to give you the news," he said, "But he was out of town on business today when the news came through, and he's been stuck in traffic ever since. He's personally requested me to come here tonight and tell you all the good news, and good news has never felt quite like this."

He cleared his throat.

"My friends, our day has come," he said, "Today in Parliament, the British government overturned the abortion laws! *Abortion is now illegal!*"

The place erupted. All were shrieking in delight, applauding and cheering. Some began to climb up on the tables to dance out their happiness, but Matt had more to say.

"Of course, there is one matter which we should broach!", he called out.

The partying died down a little.

"Before we've had very much more to drink," he continued, "It might be as well to hear the whole story!"

They settled into a quiet, happy muttering.

"The law which was passed today was a form of compromise," he continued, "Basically we have pushed the government to the point at which they have had to acknowledge us and submit to our great purpose, but they also have to allow for the main problem which leads women to seek abortions - that of money."

The crowd was silent.

"So many young women who fall pregnant without meaning to, are not fiscally prepared to bring up children," Matt announced, "And so, with our support, the problem has been overcome!"

Now, the silence was uncertain.

"As long as the Pro Life Brigade are prepared to support all fiscally unprepared mothers with the upbringing of their children, the right of abortion will never again become legalised in this country!", Matt cried, victoriously.

The silence bit into its own uncertainty, as elements of the audience began shuffling, uneasily in their seats, and speaking in worried tones to their neighbours.

"I realise this is short notice," said Matt, "But I know that we can expect at least a hundred pounds from each of you, up front. Come on now my friends, let's dig deep and save lives!"

The audience were no longer happy in the slightest. An angry murmuring was getting up, and people were gesticulating furiously towards Matt. Meanwhile, two cameras upon his breast, and four more on the shirt buttons of his friends, were recording all manner of fearsome reactions, whilst the three separate microphones were gathering many golden snippets of outraged conversations being conducted around the hall.

"In addition to this," Matt continued, "We have in our possession more than thirty frozen foetuses which were aborted in the last few days before the law was passed - and they all still have the chance of life if we can get enough young women to bear them."

The crowd was momentarily muted by this concept. Then Matt pulled out a jar. The jar contained something stringy and pink, which floated within clear liquid.

"We've got another two and a half dozen of these poor little beggars," he announced, open-eyed and earnest; "All young ladies willing to consider this noble venture, should come to the front where my friend will be taking down names."

The crowd was furious now, and Matt decided to leave the stage. As he leapt for the side alley, the hailstorm of random abuse, food and even a few bottles descended upon his path. He legged it down the aisle covering his head and was joined by Rob, who led him out through the pillars and into the hotel corridors.

Hazza, on the other side of the room, followed them out at a more leisurely pace. He was both unknown and smartly dressed, which made this easy. His cameras caught the fury which followed his friends to the exit, with startling clarity.

When the three of them reached the foyer, there were other big men descending upon them, but fortunately for them they evaded capture by dodging into and through an outgoing crowd of partygoers.

The van had pulled up outside the hotel entrance not two minutes earlier. They piled into the back and their getaway driver Simon blasted off down the road at breakneck pace.

They had done it!

When the four of them gathered later on with their conspirator, network co-ordinator and report recorder, Jody, back at their base, the next two weeks were largely spent putting together the interactive DVD-ROM of their exploits. This included the footage of all six cameras along with a perfectly-integrated soundtrack and interviews with the five of them, each describing his part in the project. There were also the initial conception plans - crudely drawn sketches of the ballroom layout; the details of the budget for the suits, the bribery, the cameras, microphones, transmitting equipment and the DVDs. Everything from the project was included on the DVD collaboration, including footage of Rob's cat eating the 'embryo' at the party after their escape. All five students obtained a first-class degree in art. The protestations of certain newspapers also helped the previously unknown young men on their way to lucrative and notorious careers.

...based on an idea my father gave me...

Pot of Gold

Derek Heaton walked hurriedly down the street, dodging
through the throng of Saturday shoppers. He was in danger
of developing the pedestrian strain of Road Rage as he was
continually held up and swamped by them. He was forced to
slow down, to let people pass, to squeeze though what little
gaps there were, and also to dodge small, chocolate-stained
children whose parents didn't seem to have any form of
control over them. Conscience, he told himself; be calm!
Conscience is all that separates us from the animals...

His briefcase banged against his leg, so with a silent curse he
tried holding it a little further away from him. He was
hungry too, but his physical hunger would have to wait.

Not far now. He was almost certain that no-one even knew
what he'd just managed to accomplish. He had to keep
things that way for just a little while longer, until he could
finish his task. Once he had done, once the material was out
on the internet, it would no longer matter if they took him.

Once he had told the rest of the world what he knew, the
world would be forced to change.

Heaton dared not hold the case to his chest, although his
instincts told him to. He didn't need to draw any

unnecessary attention onto himself. He cursed when the case banged against a car as he passed it. He looked around him, quickly. No-one was watching him, nor following him. He had no need to panic. He set off again, trying not to run. Just keep moving, he thought to himself, nearly there...

He got to the big old house and entered, cautiously. He turned the lights on, and the place seemed empty. His heart hammered in his chest and he breathed heavily. He shut the door behind him and locked it. Then he ran up the two flights of stairs to his flat, on the top floor of the house.

He entered the flat with yet more caution than he had entered the house. He stood in the tiny hallway and turned its light on, and those of the three other rooms. He then checked each room in turn, locking their windows shut as he did so. He returned to his miniature hall and looked out of the open door onto the landing.

No-one greeted him. Silence battered his eardrums.

He shrank back inside and locked the door behind him. He was safe, or at least, as safe as he could be.

He turned off all the lights except for the one in the living room, which he now entered again, shutting the door firmly behind him. This room was reasonably spacious, allowing Heaton room for a couple of small couches, a modest desk - the surface of which was almost completely taken up by his computer and its peripherals - and at the other end of the room was a medium-sized double bed, half of which was very seldom used.

Files, paperwork and books littered the shelves and half of

the floor. When he wasn't at work in the office, Heaton spent most of his life in here.

After he'd locked the windows and drawn the curtains, Heaton started up his computer and then turned the light off. The glow of the monitor was enough for him to see by. Normally he would have put some music on to relax him and make his work flow more easily, but not today.

The system was ready. Heaton began scanning the material. There were only so many pages he needed to feed into the scanner, but the wretched machine seemed to work ever slower. As for his computer... well. Two years ago it had been top of the range but now, although he hadn't tried to feed very many upgrades into it, and although the hard drive was less than half-full, the damned thing took ever longer to perform simple tasks. Tasks which, he thought grudgingly, always seemed reasonably quick upon the inferior computer on his desk at the office. Each image was taking so very *long* to appear on the screen. Even when the scanner had completed its task, the 'Portals' operating system would invariably um and ah and tick and tock to itself for interminable periods afterwards, until the image finally dribbled onto the monitor screen and could be saved.

While he was pondering these irritating facts, and his machines whirred away, he found himself wondering what would become of the 'Portals' parent company, Digicore, in the new world he was about to create. The governments of the world would be forced to retake control, forced to place some limits on the corporations, surely? In the face of the bombshell he was about to drop, the world could only grow fairer and more humane. There would be no alternatives.

There couldn't be, could there? Not against the scientific evidence he had acquired, he was certain.

It wouldn't even matter if the story was ridiculed by everyone in the media, by every politician, every judge, every barrister, businessman and every person imaginable; because the seeds of doubt would have been sown. After the whisper was out, every downtrodden soul and everyone who cared about the inequality and hypocrisy of the world would undoubtedly suspect the story of actual plausibility. It would surely lead to scientists everywhere doing research of their own.

God bless the internet!

But of course, what he knew might inspire civil wars across the globe, were it to be released without warning. Would 'God' bless that?

Heaton shook his head. It didn't matter; there was no God. Besides, when he realised what it meant to live when he knew something as terrible as this, he couldn't face it alone. It was a lot for someone of a mere twenty-two years to take in. Perhaps if others were forced to realise it, there would be some leeway given. A chance for people to come together and cease this pointless, divisive, global competition.

He was halfway there. He'd been scanning the material and daydreaming for nearly an hour. He began converting the images he had taken into files of optimum capacity for the website, while others were still being scanned.

The thoughts raced through his head; the imminent success, the triumph, the spectacular end to the lies and the injustice of the world. He, Derek Heaton, would begin the glorious 'End to Evil.'

The creation of the website, including the scanning and file optimizations, had taken about two and a half hours. No-one had called for him in all that time. His fear had subsided. He could feel his success. The sweet smell was in the air already. It was ready. All he had to do was upload it onto the internet, and advertise it briefly in a few choice locations.

The Internet connection failed. Heaton banged his desk in frustration, causing the contents to rattle, and the dirty wine glass fell off. Luckily, it landed on the bed.

He tried again, and failed again. After hours of paranoid silence a couple of floppy disks crashed to the floor, as Heaton found himself the victim of a minor bout of Tourette's Syndrome. Then he calmed himself once more. 'If at first you don't succeed...'

Third time unlucky, and a couple of picture frames were inadvertently smashed. Heaton went to the kitchen and grabbed a beer. He hadn't meant to drink anything until his mission had been accomplished, but what the hell. He was one step away - he just needed the connection to work. It had never failed him before.

He took several swigs of beer, then thought his previous thought once again. The connection had never failed him before. He'd never had to try it more than twice to establish a link to the internet. Today, he was already onto his fourth attempt. He nearly dropped the can. His heart was racing as he hurried back into the living room.

Focus, he told himself. Check the connections. First; the phone line. He lifted the receiver, and heard the usual dialling tone. The problem wasn't there, so it must be a connection somewhere between the phone socket and the computer CPU.

He put the receiver back, and was startled as the phone immediately began to ring.

Fear seized him. For a moment he almost choked, wondering who it was. He looked around his room to ensure his solitude, then answered.

"Hello?"

"Hello Mr Heaton," said a smooth, self-assured voice.

"Who is this?", Heaton demanded.

"Who are you, Mr Heaton?", the voice crooned, "Or should I ask, as my superiors would have me ask; who the *hell* are you? Who the hell are you to imagine that you can get away with the act of terrorism that you are currently trying to commit?"

Heaton felt the blood drain from his face. His guts wrenched at him, and he had to stifle the involuntary gasp.

In the seconds it took him to collect his thoughts, the voice spoke again.

"I'm sorry Mr Heaton," it said, soothingly, "Did we catch you off-guard?"

"We?!", Heaton spluttered, "Who's 'we'? Who are you?"

"Who I am is unimportant, Mr Heaton, but just to put you at your ease, my name is Douglas Hellman. Now you and I really need to meet face to face, Mr Heaton."

Heaton was at the window, inching back the curtain slowly. The street below was empty of anything suspicious.

As he grabbed his coat, Heaton growled at Hellman as fiercely as he could,

"Stay away from me!"

Laughter. Douglas Hellman was laughing at him. It was an uproarious laugh, the laugh of total hilarity, perfect clarity and of ultimate superiority.

Heaton found himself screaming, "Stay away from me!"

"Come now, Mr Heaton," Hellman continued, "You're repeating yourself and you're starting to sound paranoid. There really is no need, you know. No-one is going to come after you."

"Yeah, right," Heaton replied, "I know what you're doing. You're keeping me talking so your goons can get to me. Well it won't work!"

"Mr Heaton!", Hellman cried, imperiously, "You're quite wrong! We're not after you because we don't need to be after you. We've ensured you can't use the internet from your current location, we've used your connection line to infect your computer with a virus which should have wiped your entire hard drive clean in about thirty seconds and most importantly, we've got your family."

The room turned sideways. The fear. The faces of his mother, his father and his little brother all flashed before him as he reeled back against the wall. His parents. His little brother, just taking his GCSEs...

Then the room turned red. The anger. When he put a face to Hellman's voice, he would rip the two asunder and force that hateful face up the body's own arsehole.

The room settled, and looked down upon him without mercy. The guilt. What torments awaited his every waking moment from here on in? Right or wrong, when all said and done it was, and always would be, *his fault*.

Heaton hung up abruptly, then rang his parents. He got a ringing tone. It rang and it rang. He waited perhaps one minute, the ringing tone competing with his heartbeat in his eardrums, before giving up.

He sank to his knees, the tears welling up.

"NO!", he screamed, "NOOO!"

He forced himself up. They weren't necessarily gone. Not yet.

The moment he burst out of the flat, the shadows came alive behind him. Heavy hands were clamped over his mouth, his arms were seized in vicelike grips and the drugs were injected. The swirling darkness overcame the panic, the terror and the pumping adrenaline.

Heaton's flat was thoroughly searched, while his unconscious body was tightly bound and removed from the building. The sought-after documents were found in the bag Heaton had been carrying when he left the flat, and no copies were found anywhere. His hard-drive was already wiped.

***

Heaton awoke as the cold water splashed onto his face. He coughed and spluttered, and found himself tightly bound to the hard, wooden chair he was sitting in. Then, two fierce beams of light burst forth though the gloom and shone directly into his face.

"Nice to meet you in person," said a familiar voice.

Heaton's fear rose in his chest as if ice was rushing through his veins.

"Hellman?", he croaked.

"The same. How are we feeling?"

"Where am I?"

"You're safe Mr Heaton, and that's all you need to know."

Heaton shuddered. He looked around the room, yet couldn't make out much through the glare of the beams in his eyes. He could just make out the fact that the walls were bare. Concrete. Two guards decked out in black, stood by the huge, metal door, and he couldn't see their faces.

"Safe from whom?", he asked.

"Yourself. The material you obtained has been destroyed, as has your computer's hard-drive. You have no evidence against us anymore."

They had it all figured out, didn't they? But memory was returning now, and...

"What have you done with my family?", Heaton demanded.

"Ah, you see; there's the problem. Your parents, unfortunately, were both killed in a fatal car crash."

Heaton's horror writhed within him. The tears were coming, and through the raging thoughts scouring his brain, he could vaguely hear Hellman, chuckling at him.

He screamed. A host of vile obscenities swarmed incestuously over one another as he spat out his venom at Hellman, who only chuckled the louder.

Suddenly, Hellman was deadly serious. "Enough," he commanded, "Surely you knew what your discovery would be worth, if you ever tried to bring it into the light? We had to take those closest to you, to make certain, you understand. We've spared your little brother, for now."

Heaton was past hearing him. His muttered threats of abominable vengeance were choked by his sobs.

"Mr Heaton!", Hellman cried, "I said your brother is still alive and well! Do you want him to stay that way?"

Through the pain and the poison; hope. He had to look after his little brother, and he still could. He just had to concentrate.

"Where is he?", Heaton managed to gasp.

"He's as safe as you are, perhaps more so. His life is now in your hands."

Heaton took a deep breath. "What do you want?", he asked, quietly.

"You know perfectly well what we want. We want to know for certain that the material you stole has not touched, and cannot touch, the hands of any other person who lacks the proper clearance."

"What? You're mad!", Heaton cried, "I took the papers straight home! I didn't tell anyone - how would I have known who to trust?"

Hellman stared straight into Heaton's eyes, and held the gaze fast. Heaton stared back in shock. Those eyes, boring into his very essence, seemed endless. Like black holes, the eye's of a mannequin.

"For God's sake!", Heaton screamed, "Please! You have to believe me - think about it - what would you have done? Wandered down the street telling people? Do you think I'm insane? I might not have made it back to my flat alive - please, just let him go. Let him go!"

Heaton's desperation was sending him mad. Still, Hellman stared into his face.

"Yes," Hellman said, after a while, "I believe you."

He pulled out his mobile phone and rang someone up. "Sanders? Affirmative, delete the boy."

"WAIT!", Heaton screamed, at which Hellman looked at him with pity.

"Sorry," he said, gently, "But unfortunately your little brother's captors made a bad job of it, and he became aware of us. We can't allow that knowledge to anyone without the proper clearance, as I said before."

"STOP!", Heaton begged, horrified, "You said he'd be safe! *You said he'd be safe!*"

"I did, didn't I?", Hellman mused as he put away his phone.

Aghast, Heaton sagged in the chair. Then with fury, he fought against his bonds, screaming as he did so. If he could just get to Hellman, if he could pound that hateful face into mush, squeeze out the man's eyes, hack him up as slowly and methodically as he had destroyed Heaton's life, if he could just get free...

The sweat and the tears were dripping as one from his face, as Hellman brought out the needle. There was no escape. The bonds that lashed him to the chair weren't giving an inch.

"Heroin, Mr Heaton," Hellman announced as he poised the needle close to his eyes, "You see, in the light of your parent's death, you inadvertently took an overdose whilst trying to lose yourself and forget. It was a tragedy."

All Heaton's screams, his curses, his threats and his pleas went as if unheard. The cold steel of the needle entered his arm with steady precision, then came the rush of cool liquid into his vein. He was dead. He grinned at Hellman.

Hellman stared in shock at his catch. The rush would take a couple of seconds, but Heaton had grinned straightaway.

He grabbed Heaton's face roughly, and said, "What the hell are you grinning at?"

"Bad luck!", Heaton murmured, still grinning. Then the madness hit him like a tsunami, speeding through his head, sending him insane, and finally carrying him away...

"Damn!", Hellman yelled, "We must have missed something!"

He turned to the guards, while Heaton's body was still convulsing and dribbling in the chair.

"Get me Ericson, and get him now!", he commanded.

***

"No!", said Ericson in agitation, "He went straight from the complex back to his flat."

Hellman was towering over Ericson, one of the five Monitors keeping tracks on most of the city centre, as well as many other urban areas, at a huge panel of more than two-hundred small TV screens. It was commonly agreed amongst the lower orders that the room was too low-lit, but this was never questioned. It was meant to be a depressing atmosphere. The dingy, grey, metallic walls only made the dullness sharper. This was to encourage the Monitors to work ever harder, both to ensure the best possible chance of a quick promotion out of the Monitoring Room, and to see to it that the monitor screens were the only interesting things in the room to look at. Fraternisation with each other was not encouraged, and the Monitor Room was also Monitored.

Hellman stared at Ericson, his death-dark eyes shimmering. Ericson felt the hairs on the back of his neck rising. He had never seen Hellman so weird - it was almost as if he was scared.

"Straight home?", Hellman enquired, in friendly tones, "He went straight home?"

He leaned in close towards Ericson who couldn't help but swallow, as the foul scent of Hellman's breath wafted relentlessly into his nostrils. The Monitor had never before felt the silent, lurking intensity of the grave boring into him from such close quarters. The terror he felt was becoming total, the urge to run was pressing him more and more, yet he was even more scared at the thought of avoiding Hellman's eyes.

A slow smile spread across Hellman's features, and Ericson couldn't help but shiver.

Hellman's smile vanished abruptly. "Are you certain?", he growled, "Can you demonstrate to me, beyond doubt, that Heaton could not possibly have duplicated this information and sent it to anyone else? You have him on CCTV, all the way from the complex to his flat?"

Ericson faltered, and before he could help himself his eyes dropped under Hellman's fearsome gaze. At this, Hellman smiled once again. He pulled out his cosh and used it deftly, to smash Ericson's nose into splinters.

Ericson fell to the floor, squealing and clutching his face. At a nod from Hellman, one of his black-clad, impassive guards dragged Ericson from the room, whimpering, and dripping with blood and mucus.

The four remaining monitors at the control board - three men and a woman - all concentrated determinedly upon their work, as Hellman sat down in Ericson's seat. He looked around him and took note of the Monitors' behaviour with amusement. The guard returned and quietly motioned his request for a decision concerning Ericson. Hellman motioned him to wait.

"Now then," Hellman said to the other Monitors, "Relax, it was Ericson's responsibility, not yours. But right now, we have work to do. I want all footage of Heaton from the moment he left the complex, to the moment he got home."

The Monitors looked at each other. Murfield and Denver looked each other in the eye, then looked slowly away. The other man, Whitfield, eyed his surroundings nervously, lending their other colleague, Sarah Myers, no support at all. Myers saw her chance to take the initiative.

"The footage is on V-drive sir, shall I play it now?"

"Have you seen it?", Hellman asked.

"Yes sir,"

"Are there any gaps in the footage?"

Myers hesitated, then,

"Yes sir," she replied.

Seeing her fear, Hellman said, "Relax. It's like I said, Ericson was the one in charge. Any mistakes were down to him. Now, rather than having to sit and watch forty minutes of footage of a man with a rucksack walking home through the Saturday shoppers; what can you tell me?"

Myers looked at her colleagues, who remained mute.

"Well sir," she began, "Heaton was on screen for at least thirty-four of those minutes, but there aren't any surveillance cameras on Brook Street."

"So he took about six minutes to walk along the street?"

"Yes sir."

"In your opinion, how long should he have taken?"

"Well, about six minutes sir - that's the assumption that Ericson made, that's why he didn't think it was worth mentioning."

"I see," Hellman replied, grimly, "Right. I want to see the footage beginning at precisely the moment when Heaton was relocated after the six-minute gap."

"After, sir?"

"You heard me."

Myers took a few minutes rewinding and fast-forwarding the footage, then she paused it."

"That's it sir," she said.

Hellman was standing behind her chair, arms folded.

"Play it," he said.

On the screen, the flickering buildings resumed their pixelized reality. Figures caught in mid-step continued walking, trees began swaying in the breeze and the traffic resumed its unsteady rhythm.

"There!", said Myers, pointing at a figure on the screen who had just emerged from behind a row of buildings.

"Freeze it!", Hellman barked.

The screen froze. The small, blurry figure which Myers had indicated was far from clear.

"Zoom in on him," Hellman ordered.

Myers did as asked. She selected an area of the screen just around Heaton's figure, and zoomed in upon it. The frozen image then took a few seconds of interpolation, to clarify properly.

Hellman frowned. "Too pale. Decrease the brightness fifteen percent, increase contrast by twenty-five per cent, colour ten per cent, and zoom in on his head and shoulders," he said.

Myers obeyed. Heaton's head and shoulders were slowly

brought into clear view. He looked a little flushed.

"Keep this view," Hellman ordered, "Take it back ten seconds and set the program to track him."

The screen flipped back, then focused on the spot from which Heaton had appeared. A second later Heaton came round the corner, sharply. He looked a little flustered, but as he walked out into the field of the camera, he glanced directly at it, then quickly away again.

"Little bastard!", Hellman murmured to himself, "Obviously much cleverer than anticipated. Should have played the brother for a bit longer..."

"Sir?", Myers looked at him.

"I want to know what's on that street; what shops and other facilities."

"Yes sir," Myers replied. She opened her computer directory, brought up Brook Street and began reading:

"Pricewatch Plonk - off-licence, Arthur's News - newsagents and tobacconist, King Balti -"

"Stop!", Hellman interrupted, "This newsagents - can you buy stamps there?"

"It doesn't say," Myers answered, "But there is also a Post Office."

Hellman clutched his brow. "So envelopes and stamps are covered," he said, "Now, does this newsagents have a photocopier?"

Myers had realised where this was going, and as a result was very uneasy. However, she knew she wasn't going to avoid the storm by delaying it.

"Yes sir, I'm afraid it does."

"God damn it!", Hellman exploded, "That's it then. He knew it all in advance - all he had to do was take the copies and send the material. That, and make sure he made it from one end of the road to the other in about six minutes. He was a young man, that would have been no problem... "

Apprehension gnawed at the spines of the four Monitors, as Hellman descended into venomous muttering to himself.

Just when they were getting used to this, he made them all jump by screaming,

"FUCK IT!"

Everyone looked down in silence, but Hellman had ceased his shouting. He looked at the statuesque guard, who was waiting as patiently as the gunmetal walls, and gave him a none-too-discrete hand signal. The guard nodded, and left.

The Monitors looked at each other in horror.

"Right," Hellman announced, oblivious, "I need all the post in every post box on that street searching through. We need a list of all likely media contacts Heaton may have used, as well as all Heaton's friends and relatives. Any of the mail that matches any name on that list - I want brought directly to me - understand?"

"Yes sir!", Myers replied, "I'll have the Rookies right onto
it."

"I want results within two hours," Hellman declared, his eye
on her name-tag, "Myers!", he added.

***

One hour and nine minutes later, the two least able, most
irritating Rookies, Alfie and Bingo, were about halfway
through the piles of post.

"I hope you know that this is your fault," said Alfie to his
companion.

Bingo giggled as he whipped through his share of the post,
carelessly. "Yeah, sorry!", he grinned.

"You think it's fucking funny?", Alfie said, angrily, "We're
stuck here wading through this shite, everyone else is
looking down their noses at us, and you think it's funny?!"

"Ah, come on," said Bingo, "We'll get finished on time.
We've already found six or seven fitting the names on the
list - why are you so bothered?"

"I'm bothered, Bingo, my so-called-mate, because we're
supposed to be part of the most covert operations team in the
country, and here we are sorting the bloody post, that's why
I'm bothered!"

"Look, it must be a fairly important job, so let's just get it done."

"I still can't believe you got us into this mess," Alfie grumbled.

"How was I supposed to know she was going to wake up? Come on; how?"

"For God's sake man!", Alfie cried, "We caught Myers napping! Myers, man, *Myers*! That could have really been worth something! But oh-no! Not with Bingo around! No, instead of trying to make money out of it, or a good career move, you stick your baton through your fly-hole, into her mouth and try to take a picture?! What did you think was going to happen? You're a fucking moron! I've got no idea why I hang around with you!"

"That's nice!", Bingo exclaimed, "Perhaps it's 'cos no-one else'll hang around with *you*!"

Both looked away in anger. There was a stony silence as the two continued their work.

Twenty minutes from the deadline, Alfie said, "Are we checking addresses as well, or just names?"

"Names, why?"

"Oh, I thought I recognised this address from somewhere, that's all."

Bingo sighed. "Is the name on the list?"

"No, but -"

"Well chuck it in the checked pile, we haven't the time," Bingo interjected.

"I s'pose we've got nine or ten now, anyway," Alfie said, as he lobbed the envelope into the checked pile.

***

Five minutes from the deadline, Myers paged Hellman to let him know the search was complete. The eleven possible pieces of post were sent directly to his office, along with the list of names. The remaining piles had been returned immediately to the post office to resume their delivery.

Ten minutes after the deadline, Myers was standing fearfully outside Hellman's office, knocking on the door.

Hellman called her into his large, yet sparsely decorated, office. There was a desk and a few chairs, a cabinet, a few shelves half-full of files and a couple of small windows. The room was a little too dark, and was basically designed to make people feel uncomfortable. Hellman wanted it that way in order to maintain the upper hand when dealing with subordinates.

He waited until Myers had shut the door, before saying anything. He began with,

"Well, Myers, where is it?"

Her eyes grew wide with fear. "Isn't it there?", she asked.

"Do you think I'd be asking you that question if it had been here?", he replied, gesturing at the pieces of opened post upon his desk.

Myers looked around her quickly. "I - I...", she began, but he silenced her with a grin and a wave of his hand.

"Don't worry," he said, getting out of his chair.

He walked slowly around her, looking her up and down, saying, "You did your best, I'm sure."

Myers was visibly trembling, but remained rooted to the spot. Hellman leaned in close to the back of her neck, and smelled her hair.

"You did do your best, didn't you?", he whispered.

"Yessir!", she squeaked.

He grabbed her hand, and whirled her around to face him. "Are you sure?", he intoned, his face inches from hers, looking into her intently.

She nodded frantically. She was too scared to speak, and her wide eyes couldn't look anywhere in the room but straight into his.

"I'm not sure, you know," he growled, "Can you help me put my mind at rest?"

Suddenly, she could think of only one solution to the danger.

Afterwards, when she was trying to shut it out, she would tell herself that she hadn't made the first move, that it had been a mutual thing, and if not then it had been Hellman simply taking advantage. Because afterwards, he seemed so much more relaxed. He chatted away to her as if they were old friends, he told her things in an offhand manner that she'd be killed for, if she ever said them aloud again. He told her really not to worry, *really*, she was safe, there probably wasn't anything to look for anyway - Heaton had just fired a good parting shot at him, that was all. He also told her not to mention this liaison to anyone, ever, because it would be a terrible pity if her husband found out.

She'd had to agree with that.

Not long after she left his office, looking tousled and pale, she found herself in the nearest toilet, throwing up. It wasn't just the vile act she had so recently committed, it was the casual manner in which he discussed his affairs with her afterwards; the murder, the intimidation, the horror and the fear and, how he not only set about contriving them, he positively thrived upon it all.

Myers' make-up stained face looked pitifully back at her in the mirror, and she knew precisely what it was telling her.

***

One week later. A high school English teacher by the name of Archie Willard was sitting at his table, finishing breakfast. It was late Saturday morning, the sun was shining and everything looked far too bright and cheery. He had half a mind to close the curtains again, or put his shades on, but he didn't bother. His hangover seemed to get worse the more water he drank. Breakfast and a couple of paracetamols hadn't helped as they should have, either.

Willard sighed, lit up a fag, and began browsing his mail. It hadn't been opened for a week as he had been too busy planning lessons, marking course work and helping to see some of the children through the suicide of a friend.

The pile of envelopes was not very interesting. There were several pieces of junk mail; a firm of newly legalised loan-sharks were offering him free money, there were three leaflets detailing many of the 'spectacular offers' now on at his local supermarket, an offer by some gas company to provide him with the cheapest electricity ever and several others of a similar ilk. A few bills as well, naturally, and just two hand-written envelopes. One was in his daughter's handwriting, probably a request for funds. The other was a big envelope, and it was addressed to his wife.

"Jesus H. Christ!", he said out loud. Whoever had sent it was obviously unaware that his wife had been dead for seven years. He opened the envelope, only to find another sealed, stamp-addressed envelope within, along with a note.

Frowning, he inspected the note. It read:

Dear Mr Willard,

I'm really sorry to bother you like this, and to have to use your wife's name as cover, but I can't afford to take chances. If they catch me then this information will never get out, and it absolutely _has to_.

I desperately need you to post this envelope for me

as soon as possible. I would do it myself, but it might just fall into the wrong hands if they're tracking me.

Please, please, do me this one favour,
An old and faithful student,

Derek Brian Heaton
P.S. If I ever see you again, it's my round!

Willard leapt up, sending his chair over backwards. The name of Derek Heaton, along with the names of his parents and his little brother Will, had all been in the papers earlier in the week. They had made one of the most tragic stories of recent years; the parents had both been killed in a car crash, followed by the elder brother Derek accidentally overdosing on heroin in an attempt to numb the pain and then, most terrible of all, was little Will Heaton, overcome with grief, throwing himself under that train.

The school had been in mourning this week. Will Heaton had been going to take his GCSEs this year, and Derek was an old pupil who had been favoured by all the staff who had taught him. Few could believe that their former golden boy had descended to the level of being a junkie, yet there it had been in black and white.

Now here was a cryptic letter from Derek Heaton, dated last Saturday - the very date he was supposed to have died. A letter addressed to Willard's long-dead wife, but the content was directed at Willard himself. It had been a wilful deception to avoid detection. What on earth could Heaton have found out that was worth not only him, but his entire family? What kind of organisation could have been responsible? How powerful were they - could they manipulate the entire media?

What on earth was in the envelope?

Willard spent many minutes thinking about his situation. It was entirely possible that the contents of the envelope were meaningless, but it was also possible that it held secrets way beyond the deepest, darkest conspiracy theories around. All kinds of mad ideas raced through his mind and he grabbed the letter opener, but then stopped. If the contents had been worth four lives already, what would one more matter? Did he want to know the truth so badly that he was ready to risk his life?

Then there were the Heaton boys. Will's course work was still sitting, unmarked, in a pile on his desk. He was - *had been*, Willard reminded himself bitterly - a good pupil, like his elder brother before him. He owed Derek his last request.

The address on the envelope was for the National Inquirer newspaper, he noted with appreciation. There were no newspapers so dedicated to the truth, even though their slant was blatantly left-wing. Even better, the addressee was Bob Templeman, a reporter famed for his dedication to truth and honesty no matter what the obstacles. Derek Heaton had obviously selected the best possible man to expose... whatever it was.

Willard left the house as soon as he'd got his shoes on. He then drove five miles to the nearest town to post the letter. He didn't particularly think this was necessary, but if anyone was onto him as they had clearly been onto Heaton, it was worth the extra effort.

He posted the letter quickly, then went into Smiths and bought a CD he'd been meaning to get for ages. He returned home feeling strangely excited. What would the weeks ahead bring? He would certainly be watching out for Bob Templeman's column...

***

Two days later, Sir Luke Jameson, editor-in-chief of the National Inquirer was surprised when Bob Templeman dialled him up on the internal phone network, demanding to see him, a.s.a.p.

"Really?", Jameson replied, "What have you got for us this time?"

"I'm not telling you over the phone," Templeman said, "When can I see you?"

Jameson frowned. Bob Templeman was not normally one for paranoia; he was usually fearless with his exposes.

"Why don't you come up and see me right now?", he said.

Two minutes later, Templeman entered his office carrying an A4 sized envelope.

"Morning Bob," Jameson grinned, "What's this all about

then?"

Strangely, Bob Templeman looked flustered. He sat down opposite Jameson, shaking his head. "Where to begin?", he muttered to himself.

The editor remained silent, waiting for the news.

"Basically," Templeman said, "It has to do with genetics. I have scientific evidence here - albeit photocopied evidence - that the mental faculty of 'Conscience' is genetic. Some of us have it to greater degrees than others, and some of us don't have it at all."

Jameson sat back in surprise.

"Conscience is *genetic*?!", he said.

"Yes; genetic, and it isn't linked in any way to intelligence. Do you understand the implications?" Templeman got up and began pacing the room.

"Implications?", Jameson shook his head slowly, "I haven't even got that far yet. I'm having trouble with how you could even prove such a thing."

Templeman stopped. "Look, the proof isn't even the half of it!", he crowed, "The point is the hidden organisation that's covering up the facts!"

Jameson's clasped hands struggled with each other, briefly, then opened in a gesture of incomprehension.

"Alright," he said, "Suppose I accept these radical ideas of yours. 'Conscience' is genetic, and not linked to 'intelligence'. What hidden organisation would want to cover up these discoveries, assuming their validity?"

Templeman stopped pacing once more, and attempted to make the ideas coalesce properly. It was not easy. There had been no ultimate conclusions about the usage of this new knowledge in the material he had received; simply a scientific principle established, an allusion as to its use in the real world and of course, the name of the sender.

"Remember the Heaton family?", he asked.

Jameson blinked. "The entire family that died last weekend?", he said, "Yes, I remember. What about them?"

"I believe they were killed because the older son, Derek Heaton, found out about the organisation."

"What organisation?" Jameson was beginning to sound irritable.

"Look," said Templeman, patiently, "You know that there are many factors in the world which neither you nor I can change, no matter what we choose to write about them in the Inquirer."

Jameson cocked his head to one side.

"The destruction of the rain forests, and the extinction of indigenous species which accompanies it," Templeman continued, "The Greenhouse Effect threatening to melt the polar ice caps and submerge half of the land-mass of planet Earth; heavily enforced international trade agreements that rob the poorer countries of their rights and their already meagre wealth; Western policies that sustain wars and the Western companies which supply the weapons; the population explosion and the fact that, if everyone in the world was to live as the average Westerner does, this entire planet wouldn't have even half the resources to cope."

As Templeman took a breath, Jameson's wide eyes blinked. "Go on," he said.

"We also know that the reason for all these problems is our greed - the greed which we 'noble', rich Westerners have not only forgiven ourselves, but take for granted as our God-given right. There will always be voices of dissent, naturally, but most people don't want to know. They just want to pay the rent and get what they can from life, never mind that the future of our so-called civilisation can only end in mass flooding, wars, famine and death."

"This story is going to depress our entire readership to the point of suicide, isn't it?", Jameson asked, grinning faintly. He looked almost as if he was on the point of laughter.

"I'm not finished!", Templeman said, scowling, "The point is, why is nothing being done, other than token gestures - designed purely as and when needed - in order to raise popularity? I believe the answers are here." He pulled the papers out of his envelope and waved them at his boss, staring at him intently.

Templeman spoke slowly now, to emphasise his point;

"No-one with a conscience is allowed to take a position of

power anymore," he said.

"What?!", Jameson sat forward.

"Come on, think about it!", Templeman said, "How many forms do you have to fill in to get a job these days? How many tests do you have to take, how many questionnaires do you have to fill in - and that all comes before the interview, when the real evidence is gathered! And who do you think actually has access to the information?"

Jameson raised his hands, "Tell me," he said.

"The organisation behind every decision, in every big corporation and every government on this planet, is intent upon a general decadence and materialism. The discovery that conscience can be defined and is not inherent to everyone, is the basis upon which the organisation has really begun to thrive in recent years, because anyone even suspected of having a conscience can be weeded out with blood tests in the guise of 'Random Drug Tests'. The vital factor is that the organisation can only continue to do so as long as the general populace is ignorant of the facts."

Jameson buzzed his secretary for coffee, and asked Templeman for the papers. He began to read them and Templeman reclined in his chair, pondering the revelations he had been a part of. What possible world lay ahead? There could be wars to come, but only if the mysterious 'organisation' refused to back down and disband.

As he read, Jameson's astonishment grew and grew with every page. In spite of this, he still got up like the gentleman he was to assist his secretary, the fair Miss Peterson, with the drinks tray.

Later, as the two men were finishing their drinks and Jameson was finishing his reading, the editor looked at Templeman in awe.

"Who else knows about this?", he gasped.

"Aside from the Heatons and the organisation itself, just you and I."

"Good!", Jameson said, leaping out of his chair.

To Templeman's horror, his boss emptied the metal waste bin, put the papers in and set fire to them. Templeman made to get up and stop him, but found he couldn't move.

"Sorry Bob," said Jameson, "You know as well as I do what would happen if this one ever got out."

Templeman struggled violently, but was stricken; immobile. He tried to scream, to summon help, but his voice was choked. He'd been drugged. Jesus, it was all so clear now it was too late! When the bastard had helped his secretary with the drinks, he must have slipped something in his mug. He found himself staring, aghast at his former boss and friend, who looked upon him, sadly.

"It was good working with you," Jameson said softly, "But it also feels so damn good to let one of you stupid, ridiculous, little lefties in on the secret. Who do you think has been largely responsible for redirecting and even misdirecting you all, so often? All we do with the NI, is give the conscience-bearers of this world a vision of something better and the knowledge that they aren't alone. For most, that's all they need to be satisfied. Poor you!"

Templman was fading. He couldn't move or speak, and everything was growing dim. Shock and disbelief danced him gently into unconsciousness.

Jameson was making a phone-call, using the emergency number he'd been given. It was answered on the second ring.

"Hellman here," a voice said.

"Hello Mr Hellman, it's Jameson; Luke Jameson."

"My God!", Hellman began, but Jameson calmed him by saying,

"Don't worry! There's been no serious breach. I've got the documents and the reporter they were sent to, and no-one else knows. You'd better send one of your ambulances round."

"Thank God!", Hellman replied, "I have to admit that I was a little worried that we may not have fully sealed the breach last weekend."

"So, what spin do you want on it?", Jameson asked.

"None yet. Just be naturally shocked and just say he collapsed. Later on we'll deal with the statement at the hospital."

"Alright."

"The ambulance is on its way," Hellman said, "So go tell your secretary."

"Will do!"

"Good job, sir!", Hellman said, and then hung up.

Jameson left the room, and pandemonium ensued.

Flurrying activity occupied the room for the next ten minutes, after which the people had other places to be. The room was left empty, and the door was locked. Evening spilled into the editor's office through the large windows, and gently bathed the room in amber light.

Lying on a sideboard, amidst a collection of memorabilia and trophies, was a copy of the National Inquirer from last week. Upturned was the article on the tragic Heaton family. It listed carefully the awful turn of events, from the parent's accident through a brief, editorial-style moralisation on the evils of drug abuse (detailing Derek's demise, briefly) and finally focussing with profound philosophy and regret upon the vile, lonely, abhorrent fate of the youngest; Will Heaton. He had, apparently, leapt from a railway bridge just before a train passed under it, and after leaving a suicide note.

The article had faithfully reproduced it, word for word. It read:

Mind's gone blank

Volcanoes of ice

The rainbow sank

Into pits of lice
I'm sorry.

Hellman had been particularly proud of that one.

*...based on a story my high school English
teacher once told me...*

© H. R. Brown, 23/01/2002

nurturing

The aged Reverend Perry Paine was tired. He climbed the old, wooden staircase of the vicarage on his way to bed. The day's charitable works had taken their toll, his legs ached and he longed to take the weight off them. Aside from his volunteer work, today he had also found the time to give his flock the Adam and Eve story, along with the fall from grace and some philosophical pondering upon what it meant for us in today's world.

This particular story always left him slightly perturbed, though unsure exactly as to why this was. Perhaps he had studied it too deeply, or perhaps the story had once seeped into some long-forgotten nightmare.

He turned the landing light off, and walked into his bedroom. The aches in his body became as nothing when the room was suddenly lit by a brilliant, ethereal light from outside, through the silk of the curtains. Reverend Paine froze. His hands felt cold, fear clutched him and yet his heart leapt with

wonder. This was no earthly light he was seeing...

A latch fell open, and the two large window panes opened inwards. The light came into his bedroom. It was emanating from a diamond-like, shining sphere, perhaps two and a half feet in diameter. Paine found himself almost transfixed, but he retained some wit and this made him slowly sink to his knees, and clasp his hands together in prayer.

The orb ceased its motion, and hung in the centre of the room. The windows swung smoothly shut behind it. It hung there in the air for several minutes, with Paine on his knees, gaping at it in wonder.

Then it opened. The light from within was different, far gentler and it had a sapphire hue. Right there in front of Paine's dazzled eyes, a being unlike any he had ever seen flew up to stand in the entrance of its vessel. It shone in a lazy, shimmering fashion, sporting every colour of the rainbow in flowing hints with every movement. It looked how he might have imagined a fairy to look, like an overgrown butterfly with a vaguely humanoid structure, about four inches in height with two great wings behind. It stood angelically before him, its wings spread out above and behind, quivering and stretching. Before Paine could utter a word, the beam of light streamed forth from the creature and into his mind, holding him fast in the kneeling position.

"Don't be frightened," the creature spoke in clear images and feelings, right into his very mind.

"There's nothing to fear from me. I am simply a weary traveller who must stop on your world for a short time, to replenish my supplies. I will be gone soon, and I ask nothing of you but a little warmth, shelter and nourishment. May I rest here for a while?"

Paine still could not move, and he found his pressing desire to grant the alien its request was somewhat at odds with it holding him fast and incapable of giving an answer.

"Calm yourself," it reassured him, "I can hear your thoughts! I am honoured."

Paine struggled to arrange his thoughts to communicate directly, overcome with wonder as he was. He wondered what exactly the alien's needs would be, and how he could fulfill them, and so the alien thought, directly into his mind,

"My needs are simple - I need sugar, and lots of it. My ship's sensors detected more than enough in your possession."

Paine was pleased - this was a very simple request and he would be more than happy to allow the alien all the sugar in his possession, in return for the chance to converse a little more.

The visitor released him, and Paine hurried downstairs to fetch the sugar. Once back in his bedroom, he offered it forward to his guest. The alien caught it in a light beam, then it floated into the ship. Again, the light fixed him to the spot, and the alien thought to him,

"This is only a fraction of your sugar, may I have some more?"

Paine was unnerved. That was his only bag of sugar.

"There are eight containers full in your food supply, below," said the creature, "I would need only three of those in addition to what you have given me. May I have three of them, or must I travel elsewhere?"

Now Paine was confused. Eight containers full? Then it hit him. 'Honey!', he thought.

"Is that its name?", the creature said, "Well, may I please have three containers of *honey*?"

When he delivered the three jars, his guest received them gladly, and again held him in the light beam.

"It has an unusual configuration, this compound," said the alien.

Paine began to think about the bees in his orchard, and to allow the visitor a few, higgledy-piggledy glimpses of the processes which went into beekeeping and honey-making.

The alien seized a jar in a light beam, opened it, and used one of his antennae to suckle a little from it. Paine could see the golden colour spreading up the translucent tube, into the creature's body.

The flood of random emotions which flowed into Paine's mind in response to this first taste of honey, was mesmerizing. He had strange visions of blossoming plant life, unlike anything growing on earth, feelings of the joy of summers which lasted lifetimes, of beauty, of friendship and of love.

"This is *wonderful*!", the alien thought into him, once its senses were properly aligned again, "I must come back and see you if I pass this way again,"

The creature's antennae seemed then to droop slightly, and

Paine caught in the mind of his new friend, the thought - quickly suppressed - which said, "*If this planet still exists.*"

"What?", his thoughts cried back, "What do you mean? Why might it not exist? Are you immortal?"

The creature seemed to recede into the porthole in the floating ship, a little, and suddenly Paine was aware of the struggle it was having within.

"Forgive me," it thought clearly at last, "I am too free in my communication with you. Your race has not yet harnessed the stars to move quickly between them, and it is beyond my capacity to teach you the secrets of such travel."

Paine realised that the creature had evaded his question.

"What did you mean?", he demanded, silently.

The creature relented. "If you wish it, I shall explain."

Paine was affirmative.

The alien began thinking more delicately than before, and Paine could sense the taut, careful construction in the alien's thoughts -

"Then I must tell you the story of my wandering, which began when I left my home planet. The story begins some time ago - thirty years, in your terms. I was young then, and I still remember the worries which my sire's generation faced. Our planet was suffering more and more from earthquakes and volcanoes. The lives of my people, all across my world, were increasingly at risk. The authorities said it was an unfortunate phase in the tectonic activity of the planet's crust."

The alien's shimmering body seemed to shade itself more in tones of red, orange and yellow.

"Yet there were frightening rumours, rife amongst the people. They told of great clusters of vast, terrifying, crimson serpents, which rose in anger from the largest volcanoes, reaching for the skies and writhing around, before retreating back down once more. No-one could verify these stories, as no-one had managed to capture any images for the world to see. Most of us paid these stories no attention. Some said it was God's anger with us for spoiling and polluting our Paradise and its atmosphere, which He had lovingly created for us."

"As I grew up, the volcanoes and earthquakes grew steadily worse, and the serpent-stories became more widespread. All this activity made us forget the damage we were doing to our planet and our atmosphere. When at last someone managed to record visual footage of the serpents for everyone to see, we all began to be truly frightened. Non believers found themselves in temples, praying to Gods they had never believed in. No-one wanted to believe the end was nigh, but there were those amongst us who decided not to continue living there and instead, to leave our planet for the stars."

The creature shuddered a little.

"Many of my kind escaped into space, yet many more did not. Those who remained behind were convinced by the golden tones of leaders both religious and political, that the danger would subside and pass away, and that they would one day be able to repair the damage done to our world. I was one of the last to leave, amidst a heaving, thunderous rending of the landscape. Still, many of my friends and siblings cowered and prayed and clung to one another, on the rupturing land."

"Once we were in space, the many late leavers - myself and others, including leaders both religious and political - flew far clear of our world, then stopped to observe its fate. The tumult of the landscape was now visible from space, it rippled and tore, lava cascaded out from broken seams; oceans were vaporizing before our eyes. Then, as the planetary crust of my home world came apart, we saw it."

Paine found himself intrigued and horrified by the images of a planet's demise which the alien was feeding directly into his mind. "Saw what?" his thoughts begged the alien.

Then came the image of something enormous, something living, flailing around in the ruin of the planet.

"It was a creature, vast and amorphous. This was the explanation for my planet's ruin; it had *hatched,* and released its searing, glowing progeny into the universe."

Paine struggled to comprehend. "A creature?" he thought in surprise.

The memory came to him from the alien's mind. He could see the colossal being breaking out of the planet's crust, and writhing around in the ruins. It had no definite shape, but was pulsating with fiery colours. The memory then shifted to a closer magnification, and Paine saw a million bright red tendrils snaking out from the being's central, globular mass, and these were swaying this way and that, probing, searching. Paine caught on.

"Those were the serpents in the volcanoes!" he realised.

"Yes," thought the visitor, sadly, "Many of us who stayed nearby, seeing the end of our world, were joined in both grief and a strange fascination. This creature was almost as big as our planet had been, and it retained our atmosphere. It used this carbon dioxide-laden air to breathe, while it tore up the remnants of our home which still clung to it. Our scans showed that the atmosphere it had would last the creature about ten of your days. My comrades and I all stayed in the vicinity of the creature for two days, in your terms, before we had another surprise."

"When I first noticed the humming noise around me, I thought there was a problem with my ship. As it grew louder, and as I searched frantically for the source of the trouble, I found nothing wrong. Then I noticed the pitch of the noise was not only becoming higher, but louder. As it went on, it seemed also to diversify, as if it was splitting from one source to a few sources, then more and more. All were virtually the same, rising pitch, and getting louder and louder. I looked at the enormous creature, hanging there in space, spinning slowly and reaching out, and I realised. It was sending out the noise in powerful, pulsating energy waves. I advised everyone I could contact to join me and flee to a safer distance, but few listened. They were all so fascinated by the monster."

"With the screaming sounds growing ever louder in all of our ships, I retreated some way from the scene, and was joined by only a handful of my kind who had listened to me. Fortunately for we few, we were too far away when it happened. After the incredible, fearsome shrieking had been emanating from the beast for more than an hour, there was a sudden, intense shift in space/time, close to it. Most of the survivors were too close to the black hole when it opened, and were dragged in. Then, as we watched in horror, our creature's sire emerged from its depths, far greater in size again. It was as big as our sun and had a clearer definition to its form."

Paine saw an image of the parent behemoth emerging from a black, singular nothing, to an almost instantaneous immensity, overshadowing the youngster by a severe order of magnitude. The parent was darker in hue and better defined. It seemed to Paine that the full-grown version was similar in shape to a star-sized manta ray. He saw the creature gather the youngster up, then used some of its tendrils to preen off the remnants of planetary crust which still clung to the youngster. Paine's extraterrestrial visitor then used a series of remembered images to explain how the behemoth had quickly traversed the solar system to the sun at its centre, with the hatchling clinging on for the ride. The two of them proceeded to feed upon it for days, before the parent opened another black hole, tucked the youngster into its skin and vanished.

Paine tried to imagine how a species could feed upon magma, or infernos, or stars themselves. The images of the feeding which the alien conveyed to him, were fearsome. Part of him could not accept or believe them.

"The most terrible part of my story," the alien continued,

"Was the readings my friends and I took of the parent creature. It had brought with it an atmosphere of its own to sustain both it and its child - it was far greater and more substantial than that of its offspring. This atmosphere had precisely the same composition as that of our planet at the time we left it. The ratios of carbon dioxide, oxygen, nitrogen and trace-gases in the parent-creature's atmosphere were identical."

Paine shook his head, struggling to see the alien's meaning and yet sensing more dreadful revelations to come.

"Yes," thought the alien in reply, "We were the catalyst. A mere spasm in Nature's greater rhythm. We polluted our atmosphere to just the right level for sustaining the creature until its sire arrived. We, and our entire evolution were merely a natural process, set in place to perfect the creature's incubation. That was why there were serpents in the volcanoes - our hatchling was testing the air."

Paine tried to move. The panic was gripping him, he wanted to escape, to shut out the ideas this alien was force-feeding into his head, but he couldn't move. Like any cornered animal, he lashed out.

"Let me GO!", his mind screamed.

Immediately, he was released. He fell back onto the floor, gasping. The alien regarded him, its limbs, wings and antennae all moving slightly, here and there. It didn't move from its place, however.

Paine felt anger filling him. He leapt up and shouted at the ethereal form before him,

"How dare you?!"

The alien was silent. It seemed incapable of vocal speech.

"Answer me!", Paine insisted, "How dare you?"

Hence he found himself in the grip of the light beam once more.

"I never suggested anything about life on your planet," the creature thought, "You did that for yourself. Yet I should tell you that the remains of the fifth planet in your system bear all the signs of having met the same fate as my home world. This means that a seed will almost certainly have been sown here, too. The fourth planet has clearly been sown too, although that one has not flourished; it is dead. As for the timing of evolution on the surface and incubation within, how am I to know? All I may say on the matter is that I have visited numerous other planets like yours and mine, since mine was destroyed. Every such planet on which life has evolved could very easily be compared to mine, in some stage of its evolution. Or to yours. I can feel it in the air here too; you perhaps have three or four more generations remaining. I've seen other worlds like yours and mine, with red serpents rearing up in volcanoes. I've seen others at the earlier stage, without a dominant, intelligent species having yet evolved, ruled instead by big lizards. I've seen three such planets as yours and mine hatch open, including my own. 'Intelligent life' only ever evolves to flood an atmosphere with carbon dioxide and other pollutants."

Paine saw the flashes of two other planets. Both were

comparable to earth, or to the image he'd seen of the alien's home planet, and both were being ripped asunder; hatching similar, giant offspring.

The creature seemed oblivious to Paine's mind, which was now screaming fear and flight. It continued, "I'm sorry to tell you this, truly I am. It's so lonely out there now, and I fear nothing of intelligence will survive in our galaxy for many more generations. I fear for our hopes and our dreams. I wonder where our evolution could have led us. I feel despair when I think that species such as yours and mine will all be gone, washed away by the tides of the cosmos. I must thank you for your warmth, your decency and hospitality, you are a wonderful host."

"LET ME GO!" Paine screamed.

The alien released him and he backed up against the wall, holding up the crucifix around his neck.

"Begone, Satan!", he whispered.

The alien still stood in the doorway of its craft, not moving.

"Begone, Satan!", Paine said again, more loudly.

His conviction was suddenly stark and beautiful to him; this was no alien! The truth was clear to him now. This was the devil, sent to test his faith! The tears welled up in his eyes with the joy of his salvation - he had been tested and he had passed!

"BEGONE, SATAN!", he bellowed in triumph, and moved forward, cross held out to ward off the evil, "Leave this house and never return!"

The inhuman form of the small creature sensed the outstay of its welcome. Its wings closed around it a little, it shook and returned into the vessel. The hull closed around it, and became seamless. The windows opened, and the diamond orb retreated and left, leaving the Reverend Perry Paine in darkness.

PREDICTIONS

"You really do drink a bit too much for a man of your age," said the PM.

It was all well and good for him to say, thought Dick Lemmington, tapping his fingers in agitation. The position of 'Minister for Predicting the Unpredictable' was a very privileged one - all the papers said so. The PM had specially promoted him to the job three months ago, soon after the horrifying terrorist attack on the tube.

Since then, Lemmington had been drinking more and more to help combat the insomnia.

Lemmington spent his days working with a team of security advisors, military men and other assorted specialists. They analysed everything and everyone they possibly could, looking for weaknesses in Britain's defences. The more he found out, the more fearful he became. The possibilities for dealing a monumental blow to the country seemed endless. September 11 had already demonstrated what was possible, merely by giving suicide bombers flying lessons. What if such a person was to carry a lethal disease, and spread it around? What else could they do? When a person is ready to embrace death and take as many people as possible along for the ride, the only limits are those of imagination, science and technology.

Lemmington feared suicide bombers were lurking around every corner, mingling with the crowds he passed through in the streets and of course, on the tube. The fear had taken him to the point where he was afraid of everything he ate and drank, a fact which was playing all kinds of havoc with his digestive system. He was sure that drink was the one thing keeping him sane, and here was the PM, grinning at him in that loving way, his eyes twinkling behind his spectacles and telling him he drank too much.

Lemmington scowled, and through grinding teeth, said,

"Foxtrot Oscar."

The PM chuckled. "Alcoholic *and* a foul mouth!" he said.

"Yeah. So fire me."

The PM sighed. "Dick, we've been through this again and again. You are going to do this job at least until the next reshuffle. You know what it will look like if I allow you to step down."

I don't care what it will look like. You've spun your way out of far worse situations."

"Somebody has to do this job, Dick. It makes people feel safe."

"Safe!?" Lemmington laughed, "Do you know how safe we are, right now?"

"No-one's going to bomb Westminster, Dick, relax."

"Relax!?" Lemmington cried, "RELAX!?" he screamed,

"Hundreds of people are going to die. There isn't anything we can do to stop it. We can't search everywhere, everyone and *everything*. Our intelligence reports are not - cannot be - perfect!"

"Thank you for bringing that to my attention, Dick." the PM said, reclining in his chair. "It's important that these things should be properly discussed before I go off on holiday. My plane leaves tonight. Now, while I appreciate that it is difficult for a man in your position to admit his shortcomings, shortcomings they still are. You job description is very clear. It may be a dirty job, but someone has to do it. I'm asking you to do it, not for me, not even for your family; do it for Blighty."

Blighty? The word stared at him with the fiercest compassion, and Lemmington's eyes were seared open, more lucid than ever before.

"Bollocks!" he cried, "We might not even have the problem if you'd listened to me in the first place!"

"Dick, I like to think of you as a friend. Now, when my friends start not only questioning my authority, not only sounding off in public about it but also damn near apologising for terrorism, it's my opinion that they need to understand these matters a little better."

"Really?" Lemmington leaned over the PM's desk and stared at him, hard. "What is it that you think I don't understand?" he asked.

"The simple fact that terrorists are inhuman animals who deserve to be wiped off the face of God's otherwise clean earth."

"Gah!" Lemmington chortled, "What a lovely little sound bite! And next you'll be telling me that our foreign policy has nothing to do with breeding the very threat we despise?"

The PM grinned. "The global free market is out of my hands, Dick, as well you know. It was your little speech in the house that put you in your current job. I'm sure you already know and understand that, and I'm sure that Alice knows it too - give her time and she'll get used to it."

Lemmington's breath nearly stuck in his throat. His relations with his wife Alice were at an all-time low, and his current mindset was ruining their sex life. Did the PM know that!? Lemmington gasped, took hold of the rage and focused it.

"Oh, I'll do my job, *sir*," he growled, "But just remember when you look in the mirror, you terminal arse-licker, you shit - just remember what everyone else sees - the sad, little lapdog, with a greasy brown nose and a lead stretching over the Atlantic to the Whitehouse."

He'd done it! The PM actually looked shocked and angry. Then his brow slowly lifted. He looked down before raising his eyes up once more to look directly at Lemmington.

"Do you remember Dick," he said, slowly, "The day we first won? The whole party was just that, a party! All together, united, happy."

Lemmington said nothing.

"Don't you remember, Dick?"

"I remember."

The PM leaned towards him over the desk, spreading his hands open, palms upwards. "What went wrong?"

He seemed almost to be pleading. Lemmington, caught somewhere between anger and genuine surprise, took an almost involuntary step back. It was not lost on the PM, who in his turn, drew back slightly and waited for a reply.

"You know what went wrong," Lemmington said, carefully, after an awful silence, "It was meant to be our government, not your presidency. I for one, thought we'd always listen to the people."

"The people need to be led, *forwards*. I need you on my side, Dick."

"You need me? Shame. I was thinking of retiring."

Lemmington turned to leave, but the PM's icy voice stopped him.

"You *will* do your job, Dick. Yours is perhaps the most important job in government, next to my own and you are the best man we have for it. You will not fail. You know what could happen to your poor family in this day and age, were a terrorist to evade your net and take you away from them."

Lemmington often wished he 'wore a wire', like they did in the movies when they wanted to capture the words straight from the horse's mouth. He also understood that if he was caught doing such a thing, he would most likely ending up facing charges of terrorism himself.

With out looking him in the eye he gave the PM the slightest of nods, then strode out of the office and away.

***

Two seconds after he had slammed his limo door shut, Lemmington's relief evaporated as he remembered where he was and that he'd not even checked the driver.

"Phil?" he called out.

Phil turned his dignified, impassive face to nod at Lemmington from under his tightly-fitting chauffeur's cap.

"We clean, then?" Lemmington asked.

"All the usual checks have been carried out, sir," said Phil, "I believe the vehicle is totally safe for the minister to travel in. Where to, sir?"

Lemmington breathed out long and hard. "Home," he said, then, "No, wait - take me home via Threshers."

"Very good sir."

As soon as Phil had gone into Thresher's for him, Lemmington felt the fear again. He was unprotected. Now would be an ideal time for a terrorist to attack him. The limo was bullet-proof, but that wasn't enough. He knew it wasn't enough, he knew all about the fearsome weapons which were proliferating in the world today. He glanced around at the passing traffic. Too many cars. He forced himself to look straight ahead, wishing he'd had the guts to join Phil in the queue inside the glass-plated interior of the shop but equally knowing that he'd have felt just as scared and trapped to be in the midst of strangers with Phil, as he felt right now.

It was that bastard at Number Ten. It was all his fault. The PM had smiled sweetly, over three months ago when Lemmington had stood up in the House to argue the case to be not only 'Tough on Terrorism' but simultaneously, 'Tough on the Causes of Terrorism'.

Within thirty-six hours, he had landed his current job.

Since then, his head had become a war zone; where suicide bombers rode on one in every ten trains, buses, ferries and aeroplanes, where poison attacks on different batches of foodstuffs were reported almost daily, where mini-nukes and devastating chemical and biological attacks were carried in every other briefcase through London and where freelance computer scientists regularly made money from techno-terrorism, releasing all manner of bugs to bugger vital communications and satellites around the globe. Various combinations of the above would often raise chaotic nightmares of genocide in his sleep, sometimes culminating in the horrifying, barbarous end of Western civilisation, to wake him shuddering in cold sweats in the middle of the night.

Lemmington twitched, nervously when the door opened and sighed quietly in relief when Phil got in. He handed Lemmington the bottle of whisky.

The Rt. Hon. Minister for Predicting the Unpredictable spent the remainder of the trip home clutching the bottle ever tighter, his anger mounting as he considered his position again and again. Here he was, about to sink once again into forgetfulness, and Alice would watch him with that expression on her pretty face. The one which made him want to sink an entire glassful in one go, just to spite her. How long had it been? It wasn't her fault; she simply refused to believe or accept half of the things he told her about his job and therefore couldn't understand his need to drink so very much. Plus her demands upon his libido had always been a challenge, and under his current stress he had expected a little bit more understanding on her behalf.

The bitch.

He scolded himself, his mind pushed the word away and then stopped and took another peek. A grim smile folded his features. He opened the bottle, raised it to his lips and stopped. The smell wafted into his nostrils to tantalise him and he could almost feel the entire evening settle in upon him; the silences between them, their teenage kids quickly finding other things to occupy them, the descent, the future fractured memories, the paranoid impression of the awful things he might or might not have done, skulking just out of reach in the dark patches in his head.

He winced and closed the bottle without taking a sip. Alice was no bitch. It wasn't her fault. He needed to find another approach.

***

When Lemmington got in, she was waiting for him. He

grinned at her, peevishly and waved the bottle of whiskey. That look broke out across her features.

"Got your sleep patterns worked out then?" she enquired.

He nodded, still grinning and crossed over the kitchen to the sink where he opened the bottle and poured it all away.

Alice's mouth fell open and he laughed.

"What's this?" she asked, wide-eyed.

Lemmington leapt at her, seized her in his arms and kissed her full on the lips. She struggled with him, pulling her head away.

"Richard!" she said, "You're acting like a horny teenager!"

Lemmington still held her firmly in his arms, and was looking her up and down with wanton lust in his eyes.

"Well," he said, "I know I've been neglecting your needs a little of late, so I got myself some, erm, chemical assistance!"

Alice became excited herself.

"You took Viagra!? For me?!"

He roared with glee and kissed her again, and before long she had allowed herself to be led upstairs despite a few half-hearted pleas for restraint because the kids would be home soon. Lemmington focussed every ounce of his being upon his wife for the better part of an hour, before they collapsed happily in each others sweaty arms.

"I thought you were against using it," she whispered, contentedly.

Lemmington felt himself smiling hugely with his triumph.

"Didn't take any, really," he said.

She sat up and looked at him. "I don't believe you!"

As the sheet left them, he examined her naked breasts, not as firm perhaps as once they had been, but still a fine sight and endearingly enticing. The look on his face said it all. Alice shook her head, trying to take it in.

"So, what happened?" she asked.

"I am finished trying to find sleep through drink," he said, hoping he wasn't lying, "And I recall that in days gone by, when I measured up to your needs, I never slept better."

"Are you saying I can have it, whenever I want?" she asked, grinning, "You sure you're up to it?"

"Every man must die of something, my dear," he said, "And I'd rather die making love to you than doing anything else!"

Alice squealed and caught hold of him and pushed him down firmly, that she might have another go.

"Give a man five minutes!" Lemmington complained, but he was led into another bout. During this one, the kids arrived home and they were put off.

***

Later that night, when the kids were out of the way once again, Lemmington did his very best to wear his wife out. Afterwards, they snuggled together in sweet-smelling warmth of their king-sized duvet and Alice asked him,

"So, do you think you'll sleep now?"

"Oh yeah," he said, trying not to remember why it was she had asked him the question.

"I hope so," she said, squeezing him, "I know you have a lot of awful things to think about at work, and I know you were thrust into this job without wanting it, but you know that you really can't go saying what you said without some comeback,"

Lemmington felt bits of his body beginning to tense up again.

"Promise me," she pleaded, "Promise me you won't go saying things like that again in the House?"

"Oh, no, of course I won't," he grumbled, "Honesty is rarely the best policy in this life, and it certainly isn't in the House."

"I'm serious," she said, "It hasn't been easy on me or the kids, either. Terrorists aren't everywhere, you know. Life's too complicated already - you might as well try to enjoy it."

"I'm serious too," he said, quietly.

Alice sighed. "What do you mean?"

Lemmington felt the delicious sleep sliding away from him, but he wasn't going to hide what he wanted to say. How to say it, simply? The last thing he wanted right now was to get into a major discussion about world politics and the rights and wrongs of it all. Then it came to him.

"Look at it this way," he said, "If the Romans had discovered gunpowder, the Roman Empire would have discovered terrorism. Not that the Senate could have faced what I mean."

He felt her arms leave him. She untangled her limbs from his, turned over and settled down to sleep, facing away from him. He didn't move, and stayed stubbornly immobile until he heard her begin to snore, then stayed still for another hour before sleep finally carried him away.

***

The next day, Lemmington felt numb as Phil drove him to work. Part of his mind was screaming at him to panic, to remember what job he was doing and to think of the dangers which could be lurking around any corner. The larger part of his mind was thinking over his relationship with his wife. They could still have a great sex life if he concentrated upon her more, and it felt wonderful to know. Yet there things he could never explain to her, things she wouldn't face. Things which explained the world, things which explained his job and his fears, but which would only drive her from him. Above all it made him feel weary and old, so old. It seemed that as the years went by and life explained itself ever more clearly, it slowly stripped him of his true friends. He had learned to cope with this, for how could they have ever really been true friends if this state of affairs existed? Now it had begun to feel as if the years might even strip him of the woman he had loved for nearly twenty years. Was truth worth happiness? What was happiness without truth?

He walked up the steps towards the Westminster offices and heard footsteps following him, quickly. He turned around to see the PM coming up behind him. He had no idea what to say to him, although he wasn't going to pretend not to have seen him, so he said nothing. The PM saw him and slowed a little, smiled and put out his hand.

"Morning Dick," he said, heartily.

The PM looked his usual, reinforced self, yet there was something wrong. It sounded almost as if he'd been smoking, and yet the PM was a staunch anti-smoker.

"Morning," said Lemmington, putting out his hand, cautiously.

The PM shook his hand and headed on up the steps. Lemmington didn't know quite what to make of this, so he followed.

"I thought you were going on holiday," he said, beginning to worry, "Is something wrong?"

The PM continued walking for a while into the building, past the desk, then as they were getting into the lift, he took Lemmington quietly to one side, facing away from the video cameras and said, "There is a problem, yes. I'm calling a meeting about it today, don't worry."

The PM's voice said it all. There was something wrong, and this worry made Lemmington begin to panic. Did the PM know something he didn't, something which had kept him from going on holiday? It did not look good. It could be a serious blow if he was about to be shown up again, and there weren't many more he could take.

The bastard wasn't going to tell him.

"Can't you tell me now?" Lemmington asked, the lift humming efficiently around them.

The PM looked at him. Lemmington realised in mounting fear that the stalwart PM was *afraid*. He didn't look good.

"Dick, there's a new wave of suicide bombers that we've found out about."

Lemmington quickly expelled breath with whispered curses which made the PM wince slightly, "OK," the 'Minister for Predicting the Unpredictable' said, "OK, what the hell is going on!?!"

The PM said nothing, and Lemmington forced himself to assert his authority upon the situation;

"Oh, OK," he said, "This means I'm in trouble, doesn't it? Have any of them gone off yet, or have any been caught?"

"They aren't easy to catch," said the PM, his voice straining, "New scientific techniques have allowed them to reform their appearance, using a method known as 'Face-Patching'. With the right surgeon, three weeks and enough cash, a person can change their appearance, quite easily, to that of anyone they please."

The PM smiled as the implications slowly sank in.

"So, how do I look?" the PM-imposter asked the horrified Lemmington, then he reached, quickly inside his jacket.

BOOM.

BLASPHEMY ?

The door of the kitchen opened, and Grandma Harrison's crinkled old face lit up with a delighted smile. Her eyes were still a healthy blue, despite her age of nearly seventy years. She was still a tireless housewife; hardworking, diligent, strict and yet kinder than most human beings will ever be. Her lean, eldest son was standing before her now, for the first time in more than a year, wrapped up well against the bitter cold. He looked a little older now, and more careworn, yet still relatively young, for thirty-six. Still no grey...
He returned her smile, kissed her and hugged her.

"Welcome home Gerry," she said. He followed her into the warm, cosy kitchen, the steam billowing out behind them. Once the door was shut, everything felt good. The wooden beams lining the ceiling were grimy and the extractor fan was bleeding some of the warm air out into the farmyard, along with the mixed aromas of the roast in the oven and the freshly baked cakes, cooling on the counter.

Gerry Harrison allowed his mother to take his coat (she wouldn't have had it any other way), and then he sat down at the table, opposite his sullen-faced, younger brother. They acknowledged each other, gruffly, then said nothing.

It was up to him, Gerry knew.

"He's already spoken to you, hasn't he?", Gerry asked.

His brother Dale nodded, dourly. Dale was thirty-three, and a bank-clerk. His was a well-groomed appearance, or it would have been two days ago, perhaps. Now it was a little tattered around the edges. His clothes were creased, his chin lined with stubble and his hair was a little out of place. He had a look about him which - whilst being rare for his sensible younger brother - Gerry recognised. It was the look of a hangover.

"Was it that bad?", Gerry persisted.

"Let him be, Gerry," their mother reprimanded him, "You know what your father can be like!"

Gerry leaned back in his chair, thinking. Their father, the great novelist, famous for his cynicism, his black humour and his bleak outlook, was a dying man. Having spent a lifetime cutting and dicing people with a tongue so forked and acerbic that it had often reduced its targets to tears, if not into embarrassed retreats, Gerry wondered with no small degree of trepidation what the old git would be capable of saying now.

He poured himself a cup of tea from the pot, and offered it to his brother and his mother, both of whom declined. This silence couldn't go on. Gerry felt it seeping into every corner of the room, throwing each disjointed piece of communication into sharper relief.

"So where are Jenny and the kids?", he tried again. Jenny, Dale's pretty wife, was a vocal critic of the old man because she had been brought up by decent people who taught her not only right from wrong, but also to always give as good as she got. She had determined to instruct their two little girls to take the old man with a pinch of salt as well - he deserved nothing more. The old man had given her occasional glimpses of grudging respect for this.

"They had better things to do," Dale said, "And I told him that, too."

Gerry laughed out loud in surprise. "Wow! How did that go down?"

Dale gave him a look of disgust. "How do you think? He tried to throw his food at me, and he got it all over his bed. He's weak now, a lot weaker than he's ever been. The doctor says it could be weeks, or it could be days."

"He tried to throw food at you, and messed-up his own bed?" Gerry was grinning.

"Stop it Gerry," his mother said,

"Yes, stop it!", his brother yelled at him, suddenly, "You go up there and try to say something to make it better! You see what a filthy old shit he's turned into - you swallow that, then come back down here and try laughing at me!"

Gerry's grin disappeared. "Sorry," he said, quietly.

The wind whistled through the leafless trees outside, blowing streams of tattered, brown leaves around the orchard, through the farmyard and down the lane. Though there were no chickens, ducks or geese in the yard, there came the faint sound of a screaming goose from somewhere nearby. The lone voice was joined by others, and a minor cacophony of outraged squawking went on for a few minutes. There was obviously a fight going on.

Gerry had forgotten what a racket the poultry could cause. He mentioned this to Dale, but Dale said nothing. The two of them continued sitting, saying nothing. They should have had plenty to speak about but they rarely did, unless they were both sufficiently inebriated. It was a little early on a Sunday afternoon for that, at least it was with their mother around.

Dale pretended he was reading a paper with quite serious conviction, for a Sunday supplement. Gerry concentrated on his tea and bun, realising with apprehension that he couldn't make them both last forever. He was halfway through them as well - they could hardly be made to last much longer without his disinclination to go upstairs becoming apparent.

He'd sometimes wondered if it had been a mistake for him to try to follow in his father's footsteps. He had always been a big reader, and had begun writing short stories while in school. When his father realised what his eldest son was planning to do, Gerry had been sixteen. His father had surprised Gerry by not shouting or sneering at him. "So you want to be a writer?", he had asked, gently, "You want to write short stories, articles, novels? Son, you may think it's a cushy career, doing what you enjoy and being your own boss, but there is *a lot more to it*, than that. I can see you've made a good beginning already, but if there is one piece of advice I can give you about becoming a writer, it's this: DON'T."

Gerry had been taken aback. Fired with youthful rebellion and mindful of the fact that his father didn't seem angry with him, he had grown angry himself. Couldn't his dad take it? Was the 'Great Genius Henry Harrison' scared of competition?! Scared he might *lose*???

These accusations had washed over his father like rain across a desert, and he had given Gerry a rare, genuine smile. Of course, this had made Gerry angrier, so his father had naturally grown merrier. At the crisis point, his father had become serious again.

"Son," he had said, patiently, "It's none of those things. The fact that you'd even suspect such things of me, shows me that there's hope for you yet."

At this, he had gained Gerry's attention once more.

"The simple truth of the matter is that I cannot explain to you 'why'. If you do ever become a serious writer, you'll begin to understand, but then of course it will be too late anyway, and you'll wish you'd listened to your old man."

That conversation had taken place over twenty years earlier, and for the larger part of that interval, Gerry had become acutely aware of just how right the old sod had been. It had become something of a running joke between them. His father never failed to remind him of it with a grin, but it was an in-joke which no-one else was party to.

Gerry finished his bun. He took his cup of tea in both hands and breathed in deeply. Looking around the kitchen, he noticed the few changes which had occurred since he had last been there. A few new postcards had joined the collection on the cupboard doors. A few new CDs, a few new pieces of crockery. A new plant on the window sill, new weighing scales. His mother as well, a little older, a little quieter. But of course she was quiet. His parents had been together for over fifty years...

He was supposed to be a writer. Why couldn't he find the words? There must be some form of consolation he could give, surely. He pondered several ideas, opening lines with which he might try to reach out to her...all of which sounded infantile and pathetic in his head.

He finished his tea, stood up and moved towards the door. He felt his mother's movement's cease in the corner of his eye, and his brother glanced towards him briefly, before continuing to study the paper.

Still, the silence. He knew what they were thinking, as he was thinking the same thing. Though he was some forty years younger than his father, those who knew them both well could see Gerry falling into the same life patterns as his dad. They both ranted in the same fashion when drunk - yet Gerry had rarely got drunk with his father; he hadn't set out to mimic him. He carried the same anger for the follies and the stupidity of humanity and its hypocrisies, and although his writing explored different avenues it still expressed similar sentiments. Gerry had often had to endure long, patronising tirades from his father that, while he was adequately intelligent and promising, he didn't know nearly enough. His father had, of course, read every book you can think of.

Yet Gerry was no fool. He had seen his fate highlighted a thousand times. He had realised at a tender age that, if he wasn't careful, he would turn into his father. With this in mind, he had explored many different avenues and ways of life which he as sure his father never would have. But then he didn't really know anything about his father's youth, and was struck dumb when he discovered that these rebellious episodes he had passed through mirrored many of his father's, a generation earlier.

The moment had to happen. He moved to the door.

"Best go up and say hello," he said.

He could almost feel the release of pressure, pushing him through the door.

Upstairs he knocked on the bedroom door. No answer came, so he entered anyway. The room was dimly lit, and it smelled stale and musky. The withered thing in the bed lay completely still and lifeless.

Gerry froze. He stared at his father for many minutes, fearing that he had arrived too late. Maddened thoughts raced through his head; guilt, anger and terror. His heart began to race, his breathing quickened, the tears welled up - he was about to rush forward and grasp his father, to will the life back into him - he wasn't ready to let him go yet, there were things which needed saying -

Yet he remained motionless. Something wasn't quite right. He was angry.

Eventually, he said out loud,

"Who the hell are you trying to kid?"

The form on the bed shook a little, and a low, rasping chuckle rumbled forth, a chuckle which hissed and gasped, then turned into a coughing fit.

"Well," his father gasped at last, his voice thin and gravely, "Hello son!"

"Hello."

"Have you come to make sure you're mentioned in the will?"

"Yep. I want a decent cut or else I'm gonna throttle you right here and now."

The old man reached out and grabbed a cushion. Shakily, he held it out towards Gerry.

"No son, suffocate me. And fucking well get on with it, I'm sick of this -", but again, his passion forced him into a coughing fit. The cushion dropped back onto the bed.

"How long have you been in bed?", Gerry asked.

"Couple of days," his father wheezed, "Can't really stand up anymore. Doctor said I should go to bed, but I knew he meant I wouldn't be getting up again." A sickly grin spread across his features. "I managed to throw the bugger out of the house, before I fell down."

He sniffed, and the smile faded. "Haven't really been up again since," he said.

"Dad...Dad, I -"

"I know son, I know," the old man croaked back at Gerry from the bed. Gerry sighed in frustration. His father was not looking at him, so he didn't see the tears in his eyes.

Gerry shook his head. His father knew exactly what he was trying to say, of course. They were both story tellers. Gerry didn't know whether to laugh, scream, shout or sob. A rage of emotions with which he had never had to cope before, surged through him. His father had, once again, dotted his 'i's and crossed his 't's.

And probably for the last time.

Before he could collect his thoughts enough to say anything, his father said,

"Son, I need you to do something for me."

Anything he could do...within reason, of course...

"Of course I will. What is it?"

The old man grunted, and was momentarily quiet. Then he shifted, restlessly, and asked Gerry to come closer.

Gerry pulled up a chair and sat down next to his father. The dank, rotten smell was stronger now, permeating the very fibre of his soul as the old man reached out to him. Gerry took his hand.

"Son, if you were dying, and you knew it, would you seek absolution? Would you want your sins forgiving?"

Gerry considered this.

"I don't think I've got anything to be ashamed of," he said, "No sins in my past which I haven't atoned for, and no others which I'd personally consider to be sins, though many religions might beg to differ with me. No. No, I don't think I'd want any absolution from any holy man or woman of any faith. To accept one would be a lie and therefore a greater sin than anything I might be trying to make up for, so it would be futile."

The old man sighed with relief, clutched his hand tighter, and chuckled. Again, the laughter caught in his throat and became a coughing fit. Gerry tried not to notice the spittle which landed on his arm and on his hand.

"My sentiments exactly, old son," he finally managed to say.

"Oh," said Gerry, "And there was me thinking you were about to break the habit of a lifetime and ask me for a priest! So what are you getting at?"

"The twist in the tale," his father replied in a grim whisper, "Hinges upon your mother. She's arranged for the vicar to come around here and see me, later today. It's *her* who's looking for reassurance, not me. I don't want any religious do-gooder coming here and trying to enlighten me, set me on the 'Right Path', or any other shite - and I want you to make damn sure that no-one except family and friends come through that door until after I'm gone. Do you understand?"

Oh shit, thought Gerry, oh shit, oh shit, oh shit. Now, for the second time in the same day, he was facing a very messy situation which he was in no way qualified for.

"Has Mum suddenly found religion, then?"

"I don't know son. She hasn't been to church since I met her, but she does like to sing along to 'Songs Of Praise'."

"Yeah, I know."

"Maybe she's always carried the thread of some such belief, I don't know. Anyway, I don't want any vicar coming in this room, so if you can make sure he doesn't, I'd very much appreciate it."

"Jesus, Dad -"

"Jesus nothing!", the old man growled, "I'm on my death bed! Do me this one favour."

Gerry stood up. He walked away, then walked back.

"Dad...", he said,

"Don't try and fob me off," his father said, his narrowed eyes fixing themselves accusingly upon his son, "This is my last request of you, my first born son, and it really isn't very difficult, now is it?"

Gerry paced. The bile was rising, and he was increasingly uncomfortable with having to swallow it.

"Son?"

He didn't answer.

"Gerry?!"

"For Christ's sake!", Gerry burst out, "You can't ask me this! It's not my house! What's wrong with you, anyway? You might be weak, but you can still order any vicar out of your room! Or are you worried about the consequences for your *mortal* soul?"

"You fucking coward."

His father rolled away to face the window.

It took a few seconds of careful soul-searching but Gerry overcame his anger, and despite himself, said,

"That, father dearest, is projection on your part. The fact that I won't do your dirty work for you is not due to cowardice on my part, and you know it."

Now the old man shot him a look of venom and of fury, then turned away once more. Gerry almost faltered, but was assured of his own words.

Silence crept between them and began to nibble mischievously at their nerves.

But then Gerry's father chuckled a little, coughed a lot, and said,

"Worth a try! Never mind. You're right, yes, absolutely. Never mind."

Gerry, in his discomfort, was still looking for some kind of compromise, but the old man had already moved on.

"Have you got a woman at the moment?"

Gerry rolled his eyes, thinking, oh more shit! Why, why always with this question? Gerry looked around him hopelessly for salvation.

"Every time I talk to you - and these times have grown ever fewer and further between," his father continued, oblivious of Gerry's discomfort, "You've either been with some new goddess in whom you've been assured of the right combination, or else you've been alone."

Gerry said nothing.

"Do you want to end up like this (he indicated himself), without someone? Dying, incontinent and wretched?"

His father's questions bit into him, searching his very essence with the questions with which he had been wrestling with since he had first known the touch of woman -

"Or do you want to have someone you know and cherish, to be there for you?"

"I..."

"Well?"

"I haven't met her yet," he answered, hopelessly.

"Why is that?"

"Look in a mirror!", Gerry found himself retorting, "I want an equal who isn't going to try and change me, someone who's happy with me and with herself! Someone who'll want me but not *need* me! Someone who doesn't seem to exist!"

Again, that desperate laughter. Again, the coughing fit.

"Do you think I don't love your mother?!"

"Do you?"

"Ah. At last! A real question! There's still some hope for you, isn't there?"

"ANSWER ME!"

He hadn't meant to scream it. Not that his father seemed to notice.

"Son," he wheezed, suddenly grave, "We may not always see eye to eye, but your mother understands and accepts me as I understand and accept her. I've always loved her for that, she loves me, and I believe you know it too. What you're doing, is *projecting*."

"I know," Gerry said. He wasn't sure where the exhaustion came from, but it washed over him like the tide, inescapable, "I know..."

***

At dinner, Dale and Gerry helped their mother with the juicy joint of lamb, the rich-smelling gravy, the crispy, roast potatoes and the steaming vegetables. When they sat down, Gerry found himself wryly asking their mother if they shouldn't be saying grace.

Grandma Harrison put her knife and fork down carefully. She interlocked her fingers, and watching Gerry, she said,

"So, what did he say to you?"

"He asked me to sling the vicar out for him."

The old dear grinned. "And?"

"And I told him it was his problem - it's his house and if he doesn't want to talk to the vicar, he can order him out."

"Yeah," Dale murmured, "That's just about what I said to him."

"What, he tried you too?"

Dale nodded, smiling slightly.

"Why did you invite the vicar round, mum?", said Gerry, "You must have known it'd upset him."

Grandma Harrison's smile faded. She began eating, and said nothing for a time. Her sons began eating as well.

Then she said, "Gerry, you only die once. I know all the things your father's always said about religion, and how he hates the whole idea of a normal funeral and everything, but I wanted to be sure. I mean, like you said, he can always tell the vicar to get out of the house, if that's how he feels."

"It's the vicar I feel sorry for," Dale said, quietly.

Gerry laughed, and found it harder to stop laughing because no-one else seemed to find it funny.

Luckily for him, a car pulled up the lane and parked by the house. The hot, Sunday dinner had steamed up the windows completely, and no-one could see who the driver was.

Gerry got up, to save his mother the trouble. Before the visitor could knock at the door, he had opened it.

"Well," he said, "This is a surprise! Come on in, it's freezing out there!"

Jenny walked in with the children, to the delighted surprise of both Grandma Harrison and Dale.

"I thought you weren't coming!", the old lady cried, "How are you? How are my little girls? We're just eating, you must sit down; there's plenty to go around."

Grandma Harrison fussed around making everyone more than welcome, hugging and kissing. Dale greeted his family likewise, and exchanged a few curious words with his wife.

Though he could hardly be described as eavesdropping, Gerry couldn't help hearing her tell him she'd been bluffing all along - she wasn't going to let the old man go without seeing him again, first.

After they had said their hellos to their father and grandmother, Gerry's nieces ran over to him.

"Hello Uncle Gerry!", they chimed.

"Hello Sarah, hello Lucy," he said, smiling gently.

"Thank you for my birthday present!", Sarah continued, urgently, "I've got all the 'West 13' albums now!"

It had been Sarah's ninth birthday a few weeks previously. Lucy, the younger of the two, was seven. She was being quiet today, and sucking on a lolly pop.

"That's my pleasure," Gerry replied, "What else did you get, then?"

"Granny got me a doll house with three dolls and Mummy and Daddy got me some albums and a mini-discman and some DVD's of my favourite programs," she chirruped, "And this!"

She pushed a large, colourful book at Gerry. It was the luxurious photo-album of the wedding of Kitty and Tel, the nation's favourite pop-songstress and footballer, who had married a couple of summers earlier.

"Lovely!", Gerry beamed at her, his eyes wider than wide.

Jenny caught the look in his eyes, and watched him like a hawk, as did Dale.

"It's a wonder you haven't got a mobile phone yet!", Gerry said to Sarah.

"Mummy and Daddy won't let me have one!", she cried, "They say I can't have one 'til I'm *fourteen*, but everyone else has got one!"

"That's not true, Sarah," Jenny interrupted, "There are only seven girls in your class who have one, and the less said about their parents, the better." She was glaring at Gerry, so before she poured her venom into a scathing attack upon him, he said,

"Your Mummy and Daddy are quite right, Sarah. People who give their children mobile phones before they're grown-up have more money than sense."

"But it's not fair!", she whined.

"Oh yes it is!", he said, "Ho do you think children used to have to talk to each other? The same way you have to. If you're on the other side of the playground to your friend, you run over to meet them and talk face to face. You kids nowadays are running around less and less. You don't find or create ways to enjoy yourselves anymore - you have them provided for you. So half the girls in your class sit alone, on their slowly swelling behinds, speaking to people in other places. It's bad enough the way adults depend on them - I've seen grown-up people freaking out and falling apart, for the lack of a mobile phone! How would children react? I think it's unhealthy, unnatural and dangerous."

Sarah was subdued. "Yes Uncle Gerry," she shot back, ungratefully.

At this, Gerry found he couldn't resist. "Besides," he said, "Frying pans are so much cheaper!"

"GERRY!", Dale, their mother and Jenny all yelled at him, simultaneously.

"What does that mean?", Sarah asked her parents.

"You ignore him, Sarah," Jenny told her daughter,

"Yes, come here and let me give you some of this food," Grandma Harrison said, "It's going to get cold soon!"

"Yes Sarah," said Dale, "You ignore the cynical old so-an-so." He looked at his brother as he spoke, then pointed upwards.

"About thirty years, you reckon?", he asked, playfully.

Gerry's grin faded at the gleam in his brother's eye.

Dinner was quite a lively affair, except for Lucy and Gerry. Neither said very much until desert, when Lucy asked, completely out of the blue,

"Do mobile phones cook your head?"

After a stunned silence, three of the adults began saying "No!", and "Not at all!", and "Your uncle Gerry's a mischief-maker!". Gerry agreed with them all wholeheartedly, by shaking his head with a cheeky grin. He couldn't help wondering at his seven year old niece...

***

When Dale visited his father with his family after dinner, the old man was at his most benign. He immediately forgave Jenny for her deception, and spoke gently and lovingly to his two grandchildren. Only once did any bile escape when, having had to endure Sarah talking him through her 'Kitty n' Tel' wedding photo-book for several minutes, he grew tired of it.

"That's lovely Sarah, really, but your Grandpa's eyes are very tired."

"But Grandpa, aren't they pretty? I want a wedding like this when I grow up."

"I'm sure, if that's what you want, you'll get one, but now, please -"

"They've had a baby since the wedding!", piped Sarah, irrepressibly, "And now Kitty's pregnant again, and she's got a new album out!"

Dale, who had been watching in good humour with his wife and youngest daughter, couldn't resist saying,

"Yes, and Tel's now the captain of the England team!"

"Jesus!", the old man groaned, "Imagine being brought up by those two! What kind of weird, unnatural life..."

"That's not nice Grandpa!", said Sarah, indignantly, "I wish I was their daughter! Then I could have a mobile phone!"

"You take that back!", the old man roared, suddenly, "How dare you?! You don't know how lucky you are!"

Jenny and Dale, for once, felt no compulsion to interrupt.

Lucy shrank back against her mother, while Sarah, feeling suddenly very small and unprotected in the face of Grandpa Harrison's wrath, began to cry.

"Quite right!", the old man continued, a little less forcefully,

"You should be ashamed of yourself! Now apologise to your parents."

Still weeping, Sarah turned to find her parents waiting to hear what she would have to say. They took no notice of her tears.

Sarah sobbed out loud. Still, they waited. She felt the fear stab at her, and found herself crying out,

"I'm sorry! I didn't mean it!"

She ran to her mother and clung at her dress.

Jenny found herself in the unfamiliar position of gratefulness to her father-in-law. She smiled her appreciation at him, and gained a little nod in return.

Lucy, meanwhile, overcame her fear and approached her grandfather.

"Grandpa," she said, "Is it true that mobile phones cook your head?"

Grandpa Harrison nodded gravely at her. "That's right," he said, "They burn your ears off and fry your brain."

"Dad!", said Dale, but Jenny motioned him to be quiet.

"Maybe he's doing us a big favour!", she whispered in her husband's ear.

"Why do people use them, then?", Lucy asked the old man.

"People are lazy," he replied, "And those phones do make

life a lot easier."

"And shorter, as well?", Lucy said.

"Well, it's not strictly *proven*, true, but there really ought to be some kind of independent..."

Grandpa Harrison stopped talking, and began to frown. "Young lady," he said, "How old are you?"

"I'm seven, Grandpa."

"My God," the old man murmured, "You're going to be an extremely powerful young lady when you grow up." He leaned towards her, trying not to breath upon her, and said,

"But don't you ever let that power go to your head!"

***

Later that same evening, all were seated around the table apart from Grandpa Harrison (he had his stick with which to rouse attention, should he need it, and he needed it really rather sparingly). There were two bottles of white wine on the table, one empty, one slightly over half full. Four glasses were dotted around, with varying amounts of wine still in them. The talk was of friends and family, of holidays and anecdotes. Gerry embarrassed Dale a little with a mildly rude story about his brother's drinking days, which the girls were now old enough to understand. Dale returned the friendly fire in a similar fashion, much to the delight of the girls. Grandma Harrison told tales from the youth of her sons, to try to embarrass them both with the games they used to play, and the friends they'd had.

Upon hearing the car, Gerry got up to open the door. This time, he wasn't quick enough to beat the knocking.

He opened the door to meet the vicar, and all the things he had been meaning to say to the man, to warn him properly about his dying father's dubious temperament, went straight out of his head. In fact, he almost laughed. It was with great gusto that he welcomed the young vicar into the house and took her coat, introducing himself as he did so.

The Rev. Charlotte Thorn was a quiet, gentle-seeming woman who couldn't be much over thirty. Her dark brown hair was unashamedly long and untamed. Her dark eyes held a deep calm and her face was striking, if not immediately pretty, her voice was sweet and light.

Gerry brought her into the kitchen and introduced her to first his mother, then his brother, his sister-in-law and then his nieces. Grandma Harrison leapt to her feet and set about threatening every beverage you can imagine, tea, coffee, wine, fruit-juice, pop, even milk and water got a mention, but Charlotte was eager to meet the old man. Everyone set about warning her not to go upstairs unprepared, and certainly not on her own.

"Why is that?", Charlotte asked.

Everyone looked at each other.

"He doesn't, strictly-speaking, want to see a vicar," Grandma Harrison said, "And to be perfectly honest, it's quite possible he'll simply ask you to leave."

To everyone's surprise, the vicar smiled. "I wouldn't be

surprised," she said, "I'm a fan of his, actually."

In the moment of astonished silence, Gerry said, "Really?"

Charlotte nodded.

"Have you read his greatest work?", he asked, before he could stop himself.

"Well, I know most people go for "LINK X"," she said, "But personally I prefer "SONUDZ".

Gerry hid it well. "Thought you'd have preferred "BREAK THE CHAINS", he said, "Or don't you like the ending?"

"Well, no, I'm not too keen on the ending."

"What is it you don't like about it?"

"I don't believe religion and politics can mix that easily," she said.

Gerry was as philosophical as his father, and always warmed to this kind of discussion. He was intrigued by her remarks.

"Why is that?", he asked.

"I don't believe Our Lord would demean herself by stooping to the level of a politician."

No mouth in the kitchen (save Charlotte's) stayed closed, and none carried voice.

"Wow!", Gerry managed to say, "Do you always refer to God as a 'she'?"

Charlotte was smiling. "Why not? If you believe in God, how does one distinguish between 'God' and 'Mother Nature', for example?"

Gerry was stunned for a second, then said, "So, you *have* read his greatest work then?"

The vicar gave him a small smile, and said,

"It's a strange experience, reading you both. You both have the same themes, but you use such radically different kinds of stories to get them across."

Gerry chuckled.

"Well," he replied, "I'm sure you're ready to meet the old boy, though whether he's ready to meet you, remains to be seen!"

Grandma Harrison pressed Charlotte to have a cup of something, but Charlotte merely said,

"No, honestly. Perhaps later, though."

Gerry led Charlotte out of the kitchen and towards the staircase.

Once they were gone, Dale looked from his wife to his mother, and back again. He was grinning as wide as he could. They gave him no response.

"Oh come on!", he burst out, "Didn't you see that?! What do you think?"

"That would be a match made in heaven, or made in hell,"

Jenny said, quietly, "And there'd be no in-betweens."

"You're kidding!", Dale said, "She's not allowed to...you know! And he's never even been married!"

The girls were listening intently.

"Just because you think you know what the situation is," Grandma Harrison said, with quiet authority, "Does not mean you're right. I think it could very well be exactly what Gerry's been looking for."

"WHAT?!", Dale nearly exploded.

"*Listen!*", his mother said, "And be more quiet! That young woman is obviously a fan of both of them, but she didn't seem at all affected by meeting Gerry. She knew exactly what he was trying to say - 'read his greatest work', indeed! A man who writes for a living should really be able to say something a little bit more subtle."

"I'm sorry, but I don't think he'll ever even try to with a vicar!", Dale said.

"Daddy, what are you talking about?", Sarah wanted to know.

Lucy whispered in her sister's ear. Sarah's eyes grew wide. "Really?!", she cried.

They giggled.

Jenny stood up. "Pay no attention to your sister, Sarah." She glared at her younger daughter. "Come on, the pair of you."

She led them from the room.

Jenny shut the girls in the living room and told them to play with their toys, watch TV or just do something quietly, and let the grown-ups in the kitchen talk to each other in peace.

Sarah started playing with her dolls on the carpet, as Lucy sat down in the chair and began to look through the 'Kitty n' Tel' wedding photo book.

Sarah was deep in the middle of her preparations for her favourite doll's umpteenth wedding ceremony, when Lucy began to speak.

"Why are we always wrong?", she asked.

"What do you mean?" Sarah was irritated. She still hadn't arranged the flowers, or *anything*.

"Why did they send us in here?"

"We're not supposed to know about things like that."

"Like what?"

"Oh God, Lucy! Don't you know anything? We're not supposed to know about sex and stuff! If you'd kept your mouth shut, we'd still be able to hear what they're saying!"

"It's not my fault! How am I supposed to know what I'm supposed to know and what I'm not supposed to know?!"

"If you weren't such a brainiac you'd know!", Sarah scolded

her.

Lucy was subdued, pondering why she'd never thought about these things before. Why was there any reason to keep secrets? Why was she being punished for knowing things? Why was it her fault, and what did it matter anyway?"

"That isn't fair!", Lucy persisted.

"Oh, duh-uh!", Sarah crowed, "Life isn't fair! If life was fair, I'd have a mobile phone! Bloody Grandpa doesn't think I should have one. He doesn't have to go to school in *my* class. Still, he's going to die soon, anyway, so never mind!"

Lucy looked back to the book in her lap. Then she smiled. "Yeah!", she said, "Yeah, he is! Maybe we should do something to mark the occasion!"

"Oh, like what, brainiac? Put a flag up and have a disco?"

"You want to get him back, don't you?", Lucy asked.

"Who, Grandpa? Yeah!"

"Well, don't you know that we *can* get him back?"

"How?"

Lucy could see that her older sister was not like her. She'd need this explaining.

"Do you remember the last time?", she asked Sarah.

"What do you mean?"

"Before you were born?"

"You what?! No-one can remember being born!"

"Well I can," Lucy said, "So there must be others who can."

"What do you mean?"

Lucy was smiling, trying to sift back through her mind, finding things long-since forgotten.

Slowly, she said, "I think this has happened a few times."

"What are you on about?", Sarah cried, "You're stupid!"

"And the last time, I found out something new," Lucy continued, "I think I can do it to other people now, as well!"

"You what?!", Sarah was getting bored with her sister's weird talk

"Look Sarah, you want to get back at Grandpa, right?"

"Yeah!"

"And I think you're right - it's all his fault really, when we don't get what we want. It's all down to him and the way he's done things."

"So what are we going to do about it?"

Lucy glanced down once more at the picture book. She giggled. "I know the best thing we could *ever* do! And we'll *never* get caught!"

***

Gerry led Charlotte up the old oak staircase. Outside his father's room, they stopped.

"I should introduce you," he said.

"By all means."

Gerry knocked on the door, and called to his father.

"Dad, there's someone here to see you."

"I don't want any holy men of any bloody faith coming in this room!", the old man bellowed back. There followed a coughing fit.

Obviously he'd heard that another visitor was in the house.

Gerry and Charlotte looked at each other.

"You heard him," Gerry said, "No holy men! Still want to speak to him?!"

"Do I look like a holy man?"

Gerry grinned.

"Will you wait for me out here?", she asked.

"Of course."

Charlotte entered the room. The old man was lying curled-up, facing away from the door.

"Mr Harrison?", she ventured.

At this softly-spoken, female voice, the form lying in the bed moved slightly. "Yes?", the old man croaked back.

"I'm terribly sorry to bother you, Mr Harrison," she went on, soothingly, "My name is Charlotte Thorn and I'm a great fan of yours. I know you're ill, but I was wondering if you'd be able to give me your autograph?"

The old man grunted, turned over and feebly pushed himself up in bed. He could vaguely make out the young woman's form through the gloom, holding out a book and a pen for him.

He took them from her to write his name, then stopped.

"This your favourite book of mine?", he wheezed.

"It is, actually."

"Well now, there aren't many young women who prefer this one... Come closer, let me get a look at you."

Charlotte sat down next to the bed, and her collar fell into the light.

"Jesus H Christ!", the old man flinched back, "I've been had! Didn't any of them tell you I don't want a vicar?" The book slipped from his hands.

"Well, you did say 'No holy men', just before I came in," she said, picking up the book.

She pushed it back into this hands, and said "But I'm not here as a vicar."

"Oh no?"

"I'm here as a fan. I wasn't lying. I'd really appreciate it if you'd sign this for me."

"And?"

"And nothing. I'll go if you really want me to, but I'd very much like to talk to you, if I may."

The old man looked hard at her, then at the book. He opened it, and began scribbling.

"You're a vicar," he said, at length, yet your favourite book by me, is *this*? Why? A constant reminder the evils in society which you must fight against, or is it something more personal?"

He handed the book back to her.

For the first time since she had entered the Harrison family home, Charlotte was uncomfortable.

"It's a little bit of both," she said, accepting the book back from him, "It's a reminder of times which seemed like good fun, but which only feel shallow and revolting with hindsight... And it's kind of a warning, about the wrong signs from people, and what they can mean."

"Got burned, did you?"

Charlotte looked away.

"Aren't you going to read what I've written?", the old man asked her.

She opened the book, to see, scrawled on the inside cover,

Dear Charlotte,
How refreshing it is, my dear,
to reach my death bed and find that
I have a member of the clergy as a
fan!
All my best wishes,

Henry Harrison

P.S. You'll get over him,
when you forgive him.

Charlotte gasped. She would have laughed out loud at the old man's presumption, had he not been so accurate.

He was watching her like a hawk, and she had momentarily lost her tongue.

"Don't you like it?", he asked, mischievously.

Charlotte took a deep breath, then laughed.

"I have forgiven him!", she said, "That was a long time ago, now."

"If you've forgiven him, why are you still running scared?"

"Scared? What on earth makes you think I'm scared?"

How long have you been a vicar?"

"Nearly five years," Charlotte replied.

"A good-looking woman like you, in the prime of her life, *celibate*, for five years?!"

Although Charlotte didn't look the old man in the eye, she said, clearly and calmly,

"There are far more important things in life than sex, Mr Harrison. Were I to find a husband, he'd have to marry me before he'd... get the goods. And if he did, I'd know he loved me."

"Bloody hell!", Grandpa Harrison gasped, then he coughed, "You really got screwed, didn't you?!". More coughing, then, "What's it actually like, to go without sex for so long? How many times do you catch yourself riding the washing machine, in any given month?"

A look of disgust passed over her face, before she laughed. She should have expected such things, she'd read his work. She looked him straight in the eye, almost completely straight-faced, and said,

"I can't keep count."

They both burst out laughing.

"No, seriously though," the old man wheezed, "You can tell me, it'll never leave this room!"

"You're just a filthy old man really, aren't you?", she smiled.

"Yes," he said, before calling out, "You listening out there, son?!"

Outside the door, Gerry quickly and quietly lifted his head from the door, moved back across the landing and shouted, "You what?"

He stayed still, after that.

"What makes you think he'd be listening?", Charlotte wanted to know.

The old man looked the young vicar up and down, shook his head, smiled and closed his eyes.

"Nothing", he said, pleasantly.

"No, really, what?", she pressed him.

"There are very few women like you," he replied, "Very few who won't be intimidated by him, yet are interesting and attractive enough for him. He's a picky sod. But beware he doesn't try to win you just to prove that he can."

He coughed again.

"What makes you think..." Charlotte began, but she tailed off. Let the old man finish his coughing fit first.

But he didn't stop coughing. His face was reddening, his eyes bulged out of his head, and the sweat was beginning to pour from his pale and ragged brow. The coughing and wheezing turned to spluttering, and Charlotte, in alarm, called out,

"Gerry, come quickly!

Gerry's coming didn't stop his father's coughing. On it went. The old man turned red in his apoplexy, spittle flew in all directions, and the ragged breath he managed to take between the coughs, sounded like they were shredding his very throat.

***

Eventually, later that same day, the doctor emerged from the old man's room. Everyone was waiting outside, so everyone saw the doctor shake his head.

"He's asking for you," the doctor said to Grandma Harrison.

Her head bowed, the old lady entered the room.

She approached the bed, and sat down in her chair. The book she had been reading in here only last night, was still sitting on the bedside table... Next to him.

He looked like death itself. Skin like tattered, greying paper hung over his cheekbones. His dull, tired eyes stared forth at nothing in particular. The breathing was thin and shallow.

Suddenly, his gnarled old hand reached out and took hers. He pulled her towards him, focussed upon her and whispered,

"I love you."

Her tears running unashamedly down her face, Grandma Harrison hugged him tightly.

"I love you too," she sobbed, "I love you."

***

She emerged from his room perhaps an hour later, staring vacantly ahead, to find the doctor waiting with her family.

"Better phone the morgue," she said, stupefied.

The doctor paid his respects and left. The family gathered together around poor Grandma Harrison, and the sadness began to permeate everyone, not least Sarah and Lucy...

***

The funeral was a curious affair. Grandpa Harrison had stipulated 'no religious ceremony' (hence the Rev. Charlotte Thorn had been invited to attend by Gerry), and he had requested that everyone who attended should drink at least a bottle of wine *before* attending.

Gerry was almost convinced the old bugger was watching with an enormous smile upon his face, seeing the sorrow and the laughter heightened and intensified in everyone by the effects of the booze.

There was Dale, dancing around the old man's coffin with Jenny, though he must have been half blinded by the tears, and by the two and a half bottles of red which Gerry knew he'd already consumed. The kids (who were let off the drinking clause), wandered around causing as much mischief as they could get away with - the combined effects of this verged on a minor riot, at times. At one point, Gerry's agent hurried up to him, staggering slightly, to tell Gerry he'd better be writing twice as hard, now his dad wasn't with us anymore, ha-ha! Gerry burped in his face, and followed-up with a grimace and a V-sign. The agent realised his mistake, and backed away, apologetically.

Now, more than ever, Gerry felt the urge to drink yet more (he'd had a bottle and a half already, plus a few spliffs, for old time's sake), but he knew he'd end up on the most disgusting, self-pitying, downward spiral if he did. His mother was safely being comforted by many friends and family, so he'd better not go near, for now. There were many people he could have boring conversations with, many with whom he'd already done so, but one who might say something of consequence to him.

He wandered up to Charlotte. She was looking a little out of place, not to mention inebriated.

He leaned towards her from behind, and said,

"About your favourite book by my father, - why 'SONUDZ'?"

She turned to face him, surprised. "What?", she asked, a little bleary.

"I said, why 'SONUDZ'? How exactly could this book, from that particular trilogy, be your favourite? I mean, the other two are about the possible higher purpose of humanity - one which is consistent with core Christian beliefs, but 'SONUDZ' is about the extent of the callousness of which we're capable. How can that resonate intimately within the mind of such a beautiful and intelligent vicar?"

She was taken aback. He might be quite easy to understand, but she hadn't expected him to find her as simple. She found herself smiling. This might even be worth the effort!

"That's easy!", she said, "It's a warning sign, and it works."

"A warning sign?"

And so the talking began, but 'Gerry and Charlotte'; well! That's another story...

***

The light was fading now. Time faded into shades of red, and he no longer had any concept of it. Feelings were muted by warmth and comfort, but now...

He was being ejected! Out into cold, horrible-smelling room, nasty colour, and now wrapped in blankets?!"

It must be. It was! Reincarnation. Reincarnation?! My God, bloody *Buddhism*??? Was this the meaning? Buddhism, the true religion! The old man didn't know whether to scream in horror or shout with joy, but wasn't really capable of doing either, as his conscious grip on the extremities of his new self were rather weak.

Who was were his new parents?

The woman looked somehow familiar, as he found himself placed in her arms. She was a bit bloated and red-looking, but that face was... Where had he seen it before?

A tall, well-built man in a track suit was tickling him under the chin now, and coochy-cooing. He vomited. Yes!!! He had control of that *particular* defence mechanism...

Track Suit was drawing back in disgust at the mess on his hands, when the old man caught sight of the two of them together, his new mother and father. Then he knew who they were - they were the pair in that bloody photo-album.

'OH JESUS CHRIST, NOOOOO!!!', he tried to scream.

It was no good, he'd never control enough of this form to respond properly to any of the external stimuli...

The baby had been so quiet at first, but sure enough, after a few seconds, it was crying. In fact, this one was bawling and wailing its little head off. Eventually however, after tucking the new-born up snugly to his mother's breast, the doctor saw the infant begin to suckle.

And the last thought which Grandpa Harrison had, within our field of understanding, was,

'But I'm *hungry*!'

THE LONG ARM

When the customs officer took Daisy by the arm and asked her to come with him, she didn't mind too much. Her husband Collin didn't appreciate it and he verbalised this grumpily, but he was equally aware of the terrorist threat and of the equally disturbing threat of the label 'terrorist', so he relented. He stood hunched and scowling in the arrivals area to await her return.

The officer led her into a small, grey, starkly-lit office. An imposing figure rose from behind a desk. This figure had mahogany hair pulled into a tight bun and a police uniform tightly-fitted to her over-ample curves, though these were largely hidden behind the usual array of weaponry and body-shielding which signified His Majesty's finest.

"I'm Sergeant Shappleton," the impressive woman announced, "Would you please confirm your name for me."

"Hi, my name's Daisy Marianne Lithgow," Daisy said, "I'm not sure what it is you think I've done, but I'm willing to co-operate in any way you need."

Sergeant Shappleton gave an unpleasant smile. "I'm sure," she said, "Would you mind giving me a blood sample?"

"OK," said Daisy.

It didn't take long. The officer who had escorted her into the room waited and watched her whilst Sergeant Shappleton left to conduct her tests on the sample provided.

Daisy tried to engage him in conversation.

"Busy week?" she enquired, to no reply. She squinted at the name on his uniform.

"Officer Leopold - ?" she left the word hanging in the air. Still nothing. "Are you disadvantaged in some way?" she asked, "Or are you not allowed to talk to me?"

The young policeman gave a bored little sigh, carried on staring impassively, straight ahead.

Daisy ignored him and began texting her husband, Mike. "Not sure what they want yet," read the text, "But they've taken a blood sample."

"If you're attempting to send a text madam, might I save you the bother?" the young officer said suddenly, "It won't send from in here."

"Oh now it speaks," Daisy muttered, trying anyway. After a minute of trying she forced a smile. "How long is this going to take? When can I contact my husband?"

"All in due course madam."

Daisy tutted and began tapping a nervous drumbeat on the desk. This went on for several minutes and became a complex piece of percussion. She wanted to get on his nerves as this whole scenario was getting on hers, yet he remained detached and impassive. Daisy was contemplating stroking her breasts to see what she had to do to get his attention when Sergeant Shappleton returned to the room, her face a mask of grim certainty.

"So Daisy, would you say that you had a little bit to drink this evening?"

"Well it was a two-hour ferry trip, we had a meal and a few glasses of wine, certainly."

"Can you confirm the actual volume of wine you drank?"

"Only a couple of glasses."

"Two?"

"Yes, two."

Sergeant Shappleton looked at her clipboard. "Two large glasses, were they?"

"Yes, I suppose. The meal lasted for most of the trip, you understand. Besides, why the interest? I don't own a car, nor am I planning to drive anywhere, operate any heavy machinery or fly or -"

"The scanners you passed through set off the alarms, Daisy. And those alarms went off due to the conjunction of two detectable facts about your body; the presence both of alcohol, and a foetus."

Joy collided with horror in Daisy's head. A baby! But booze, why did I have to drink *booze*...

"I'll quit, today!" she said, "I'm not an alcoholic!"

"The presence of alcohol and your pregnancy have been confirmed by your blood sample."

"It was just two glasses and I didn't know! I didn't know, for God's sake, you can't put me through the grind house for just two glasses!"

"Ignorance is no excuse, Daisy."

"But my baby - the best thing for it is to grow up with me and Collin - we're happily married!

"The law is the law Daisy. I'm sorry."

Hysteria was building up in Daisy. "Please," she said, "*Please*! Don't do this. Just let me go and I swear there'll be no more booze, nothing but good food and lots of it; the baby'll be born one hundred percent healthy, I *swear*!"

"You're asking me to commit myself to dereliction of my duty, and in the presence of another officer. Are you taking notes on this, Constable Leopold?"

The first officer nodded at Sergeant Shappleton, his little pad already in his hand.

"I'm not asking you to let a hardened criminal loose to terrorise the public!" Daisy cried, "I'm just asking you to be a human being! I've never been in trouble with the law in my life - not so much as a parking ticket - check my record! All I'm asking you for is a moment's forgiveness and the right to raise my child with its father, Collin - the man that I love!"

"You getting all this, constable?"

"In addition to the charge of alcoholic abuse of the unborn," said Constable Leopold, "In my opinion the accused was also guilty of attempting to pervert the course of justice, and emotional blackmail."

The Sergeant's smile was a leer of teeth and triumph.

"What's wrong with you?" Daisy shouted, "This isn't justice, it's despicable! It's a witch hunt! I had no idea I was pregnant, I won't be a bad mother!"

"I've heard enough, Daisy my dear. I'm sure your local gazette will determine the status of your motherhood, such as it will be."

"You can't!"

"Constable, book this woman please. I'm busy."

Shappleton stood to leave and Daisy flew at her, cursing her for an evil bitch as she smacked her hard across the face. Shappleton grabbed her arms and the room was suddenly entered by two more armed officers who caught hold of Daisy from behind and tazered her incomprehensible.

"- And assaulting an officer of the law," said Leopold, "- A Seargent with an impeccable record who was going about her duties in a fitting and diligent manner. Mrs Lithgow, I believe you can look forward to seeing your husband again in about nine months. You can always try for another child after that."

Babbling incoherently, Daisy was dragged away to spend the rest of her pregnancy in the care of the militant branch of the

Women's Institute. She would know her baby for half an hour before it was taken into care.

THAT GOOD OL'
SAPPHIRE GLOBE

07/09/2304; 13:17

President Antoinne Bleoche of the United Liberated
Corporations of Earth and its Realms, the most powerful
man in the world, was returning home to the capital city of
Meta York after an extended vacation. The sun was shining
and there wasn't a hint of grey in the deep, blue sky. He
relaxed in the big, comforting sofa with a cigar, and
pondered which one of his secretaries he would visit first.

Bleoche's hovlim (hover-limousine) was the largest car in
the convoy; it had an extremely swish interior, the fastest
engine, the best onboard TVNet system, a fully-stocked bar,
double-bed, mini-shower and the best possible armour,
although there were no weapons. Other attack-cars in the
procession had serious fire power with which to protect the
President, should it be necessary. Protocol demanded that he
should also have had at least two Robot Bodyguards
(Bodybots, as they were dubbed) in his hovlim with him at
all times, but he wasn't in the habit of always listening to his
security staff. Hence there weren't any Bodybots, today.

Ahead of him over the hills and valleys, the enormous,
crystalline, conical complex of the city towered up into the

heavens, more than three miles above sea level. The city was humanity's greatest achievement. The other biggest cities in the world - Eurocentre City, New Moscow and Meta Tokyo - were not much more than two miles high. Meta York's brilliant, golden spires sliced into the tremulous glory of the skies, as if in proud reply to the very thunderbolts of Zeus himself. Indeed, they were built not only to withstand thunderbolts, but to harness their energy as well.

Endless, pearlised, interlocking plateaux wove in and around the mountainous, gleaming centre cone of Meta York, carrying roads, apartment blocks, bars, amusements, parks, shopping centres, games and concert arenas. The colour and the dazzle of the pulsating neon billboards formed an ever-changing kaleidoscope. The constant humming of the hovcars which nipped quickly from stop to stop through the air could be heard from miles away. Bleoche had always likened the distant, full perspective view of his home city to that of an earth bound vision of heaven, when it was gleaming in the sun as it was now.

He closed his eyes and thought back over the times he had had, these last three weeks. He would have preferred another week or two. The delights of the simple, unspoiled beaches of what had once been Greece, were like heaven. Especially so, when they were so laden with hordes of willing nymphets, who were born and bred there for the pleasure of those tourists who could afford a stay.

It should be pointed out that these young, humanesque females were not ill-treated. They could easily carry on their careers long after the standard cut-off point of thirty years, by doing stag-night gigs. Or, if they felt their dignity might be impeded by lowering the tone of their performances, there would always be very good, very reasonably-paid jobs awaiting them in the continuous-assembly agencies. Besides, they weren't really human anyway. Bleoche always reminded himself of the facts when returning from these getaways, because he could never be sure which lunatic feminist fringe group might be waiting for him this time...

Yes, it was a pity he hadn't had more time there, but duty called. Gamma Fleet would be back from the Gondor System anytime now, and the ceremonial celebration of their triumphs required his presence.

The ground shook suddenly, and the hovlim, with its distance above the ground set at a steady cushioning of thirty to thirty-five centimetres, couldn't help but wobble slightly in return.

Surprised, Bleoche ordered the car to stop. "Was that an earth-quake?", he asked.

"No," replied the onboard computer, in dull tones, "That was the effect of residual impact tremors."

"Impact?!", Bleoche cried in alarm, "From what?"

"An unidentified flying object has struck Meta York," came the impassive reply.

In horror, Bleoche leapt from the vehicle to get a good look at his home city.

He gasped. Whatever had hit the city was big; *very* big.

Perhaps one twentieth of the enormous structure had been affected, and that could mean... Jesus! He was turning pale.

That could mean tens of thousands of lives; gone.

As he stood there, trying to make sense of the devastation, a shadow passed over him. He looked up and saw one of the Gamma Fleet star ships, recognisable by its colours and crest, plummeting steadily down. Like every other ship in Gamma Fleet, and in every other military space-fleet from earth, it was considerably larger than an ocean liner.

Down it fell. Quite slowly it seemed, for something so huge.

Bleoche opened his mouth and screamed. For endless seconds he saw the fresh devastation and felt the tremors, before his scream was totally drowned out by the deafening roar. Without the protective shell of the hovlim, the sound was enormous; exploding fuel tanks and power cables howled their demise across the land, as did the thunderous collapse of buildings and structures. The great ship gouged its seven-hundred metre long hull mercilessly into a previously unscathed section of the city structure, leaving a chasm of erupting flames and cascading, heavy material in its wake.

Bleoche was still screaming as the noise died down. Members of his entourage were spilling out of their hovcars now. Four of the Bodybots made straight for him and attempted to force him to the ground, to cover him. He screamed the order for them to stop several times, and they ignored him. As he fell to the floor under their great strength, it took the rest of the human staff several seconds to deactivate them so that he could be rescued from the shelter they had formed around him.

Severely angered by these stupid devices, Bleoche pushed through his dismayed and panicking staff, roughly. He scrambled back into his hovlim and went online. Quickly he raced through the channels until he found what he was looking for; the terminals to Gamma Fleet. All were sealed off. The entire fleet was dead to all attempts at communication. That was twenty ships! Well, nineteen. No - eighteen, assuming the first UFO had also been a Gamma Fleet cruiser. All channels closed? Was the *entire fleet* betraying earth?!

Another deafening roar blew in through the open door, rocking the hovlim again and confirming his suspicions.

Bleoche's security chief, Van Hassell, leaned inside the hovlim.

"We have to get you to safety, sir!", he called out above the distant, ruinous din.

Bleoche growled at him from his console, "That's the problem with security staff - you're so well-programmed, you're forever unable to see the bigger picture."

Van Hassell grimaced slightly, squared his lantern jaw, and said nothing.

"They're not homing in on any one person, are they? They're targeting for damage- maximisation, they aren't going to try to hit us out here. How would they even know where we were?"

Van Hassell tried another approach. "What do you want me to do, sir?", he pressed.

"Stop bothering me!", Bleoche hissed, "I'll tell you when I've figured it out for myself!" He then concentrated on his communications.

Gamma Fleet, or what was left of it, was unreachable. Next best thing was the planetary defence systems. Bleoche launched back through the channels to grasp these systems and set them to annihilate all incoming Gamma Fleet ships.

The four main defence satellites were large space stations, each staffed by more than fifteen-hundred people. These armoured mini-moons; Kirk, Picard, Sisko and Janeway, all held orbit around Earth at the same height and in a tetrahedral formation, equidistant from each other. They took their names from heroes of the olden Roddenberry Fables. The formation was designed to maximise the defence capability of the four satellites and to leave no one area of the surface open to a greater possibility of outer space danger, than any other.

One of the stations was not responding. Bleoche himself was panicking now. He tried again.

"Yes sir!", came the reply at the second station, "We're aware of the attack sir; Gamma 7 - the *Excelsior* - she rammed Sisko station sir! We're all under attack!"

"Stop those ships commander!", Bleoche thundered, "That is a direct order of the President of..."

The line had gone dead. Bleoche went for the other two

stations, but another deafening roar rocked the hovlim. Forget the stations he thought, they're aware of the danger and will do what they can. But whatever they were trying, they weren't simply failing - they were also paying a heavy price.

What of the other fleets?

Alpha Fleet was engaged near the belt of Orion, too far away to be of any assistance for days. Beta Fleet was patrolling a system who's star was not visible from Earth. Hydra and Omega Fleets were even further out, examining new systems for import/export opportunities. Delta Fleet were the only possible interceptors available - they were patrolling the Proxima Centauri system.

Bleoche had the Delta Fleet commander on screen almost immediately.

"Yes sir?", the commander saluted into the two-way screen.

"Bring Delta Fleet to Earth, NOW!", Bleoche ordered, "We need you to stop Gamma Fleet at all costs!"

"Gamma Fleet, sir?"

"Yes, you heard me! Get underway immediately. Gamma Fleet is attacking us - millions of lives depend may on you - we need you here ten minutes ago! Whatever it takes, commander."

"Yes sir!", came the astonished reply.

Bleoche climbed once more from his hovlim, and joined the

Bodybots, security officers, advisors and other personnel from his convoy. The fifth Gamma Fleet cruiser was serenely powering down from the heavens.

Powerless, the elite members of President Bleoche's staff watched the pride of Gamma Fleet - Gamma 1, the *Enterprise* - plough itself mercilessly into the centre of the uppermost towers of Meta York.

Bleoche grabbed Van Hassell by the shoulder. "There were twenty ships in Gamma Fleet," he said, "Five have hit Meta York, two have hit Picard and Sisko, so two more will have to go for Kirk and Janeway and Delta Fleet can't make it here in less than half an hour. That still leaves eleven more cruisers!"

"Ten", said Van Hassell, dazed.

Bleoche looked up and sure enough, there was Gamma 3, the *Yorktown*, bearing in on his beloved home city. He didn't wait to see the results. He dived back into the hovlim and raced through the online channels to the centre of planetary intelligence, The Octagon.

General Kaufman replied to his summons, looking dishevelled and frightened. Bleoche almost gasped when he saw that Kaufman's crew cut was both wilting and out of place. Usually it was the standard by which crew cuts were set; it was firm, very short, rigidly perpendicular, starkly severe and commanding.

"Mr President sir," he saluted, grimly.

"What's the news, Mr Kaufman?", Bleoche roared over the

din of the *Yorktown's* demise.

"I assume you know about Meta York, sir?", he replied.

"Yes," Bleoche hissed through clenched teeth, "I can see it from here, and I suppose all four defence satellites are down as well?"

"No sir, Kirk is still with us... Belay that sir. All four are down."

"What else?"

"We've been hit ourselves. Fortunately the *Hood* wasn't quite on target, we've lost not quite two whole wings of this complex and we haven't had sensor warnings of any more of them heading for us -" Kaufman drew breath. "- But New Vegas is dead, sir."

Bleoche gasped. New Vegas was the enormous, gloriously-glitzy capital city of the Moon. Usually, the energy field surrounding New Vegas was more than enough to cope with reasonably large meteors, and if ever a meteor on collision course was too large - it would be located and destroyed before it came anywhere near the Moon. But it would only take one collision from a Gamma Fleet cruiser to cause a total breach of the city's atmosphere.

He found himself sagging in his seat, and an old quote from the archives found its way into his head,

"Oh, the *humanity*..."

He grabbed hold of his thoughts. "That still leaves eight

more ships, Kaufman. Where are they?"

"Two have largely destroyed the financial sectors of Eurocentre City, sir, one is heading for New Sydney and we have nothing to stop it, one has hit New Moscow, one; New Bagdad, one; Meta Tokyo with another on its way down."

"What about the last?"

On the screen, Kaufman struggled with his crackling comms system.

"Where's the last, general?", Bleoche shouted.

He was answered by the now familiar rocking of the hovlim, followed by the fresh, booming chaos of thunder.

"Never mind," he sighed, "Now listen: I want every force there is, mobilised to help the fire crews and rescue teams, I'm talking army, navy, air force, police, civil servants, any office workers you can get, and every robot work force is to be commandeered - understand?"

"Consider it done Mr President, sir!"

"I will, when I see it done. GO!"

Kaufman dropped the link.

Bleoche climbed wearily from the hovlim and stood looking at the deep ruination scarring the planet's proudest city. Vast sections of it were ablaze, exploding and crumbling. Emergency service vehicles buzzed around frantically, he could see them like angry bees, swarming hither and thither about the damaged hive.

The security men and Bodybots around him were losing the plot. They were patrolling the stationary, hovering vehicles, weapons drawn. All were scowling from behind dark glasses - including the Bodybots, who knew how to look menacing. They all seemed to be avoiding the terrible spectacle on the horizon by looking quickly away again whenever it fell within vision.

Bleoche saw the Bodybots carefully mimicking the behaviour of the more senior, human, security staff, and had to fight the hysterical urge to laugh. The Bodybots were programmed with intelligence, a learning capacity and with every training program which any officer of the elite security services might be expected to complete in twenty years of loyal service. They could quickly learn to act 'normally' to any situation, but now, in the midst of this calamity, they had no precedents to follow. Hence the patterns they were now following would have formed a kind of gracefully chaotic pattern, had there been a helicopter there to get an aerial view of them. It was pathetic. They could outwit any human, but their programming could never allow them to exceed any human. This meant that they were forever aware of - and ashamed of - their snivelling, indelibly subhuman existence.

There was nothing more Bleoche could do to prevent the damage, for it was already done. He simply stood, motionless, watching his beloved, ethereal home city, burning.

The image would be with him forever, he knew that clearly.

The enormity of the disaster was far greater than the horrible destruction here. Earth's defences were gone. The six largest cities on the face of the planet had been stricken with destruction, the centre of the Moon settlements was gone, the security centre of the Octagon was severely compromised and they had lost an entire fleet of star ships.

How? WHY???

The President thought he was fainting. The vast, towering megalopolis ahead of him seemed to lean slightly. He shook his head and looked at his colleagues.

He was all right. He looked back at Meta York, in time to see the enormous, bulbous central column collapsing down into the rest of the complex.

Everyone around him gasped.

While they were still trying to make sense of what had happened, a hovcar pulled off the speedway near them. The car was filled with suitcases, screaming kids and beach-gear. A woman in dark glasses sat in the passenger seat while the driver, a plump man in a bright shirt and brighter shorts, got out. He walked up to the nearest human member of the President's staff and, with glistening eyes, asked if there was any way in which a good citizen of the Earth could be of assistance.

The large security guard stared impassively at the civilian for several seconds, before expertly seizing him and twisting his arm behind his back. He then forced the man face down onto the concrete, despite his yelping pleas of innocence.

While the guard searched the holidaymaker, the man's wife and children piled out of the car and ran towards him to try to reason with his captor. Now, the Bodybots had a job they could do. Straightaway, they seized the poor man's family equally roughly and firmly, and searched them too.

The squealing and screaming soon found its way through the daze however, and Bleoche ran over to the captured family.

"Let them go!", he commanded. The Bodybots looked at each other, then to the human guard who had grabbed the first holidaymaker.

"Sir," he replied, realising his responsibility for the situation, "In view of what's happening, it's my belief that these people may pose a clear and present -"

"For Christ's sake!", Bleoche exploded, "Let them go, NOW! Or else you'll be fired and the rest of you (here he looked sternly at the Bodybots) will be melted down without prior deactivation, and sold for scrap."

Reluctantly, the leading man and the Bodybots released their squirming, squeaking captives. As they arose, pasty-faced and trembling, the President took the hands of the children's parents and offered them his sincerest apologies. It wasn't a situation which any of them had been prepared for, he hoped they understood.

"Well, hell!", said the man in the loud shirt and shorts, "If a man can't help his people at a time like this..."

Bleoche handed the man his own personal seal. "Sir, I respect you," he said, "And I fully appreciate your intentions and motives. Men like you are what has made us who we are. If you still want to help, take this to the nearest aid agency and offer your services. They won't deny you the chance to help."

At this, the man relented. "Why, thank you Mr President, sir!"

He retreated, whilst poring over his treasure with the rest of his family. They took several photo-images of Daddy with President Bleoche's own personal seal, to preserve the moment forever in all its three-dimensional glory...

The family's hovcar was speeding away, and Bleoche shook his head, his eyes closed. The rumbling of distant ruin still scoured his eardrums, and images of devastation replayed repeatedly in his mind.

How was it possible? Had the whole fleet mutinied? That was most certainly *not* possible. The security of the armed forces and intelligence services had been absolute for over two hundred years. Every recruit was monitored through every second of every day until at least one year of training had been followed by at least two years of active service. It would be an incredible feat of endurance and faith for a single traitor to carry any anti-Earth Realms philosophy and purpose through all of that, unspoken and unnoticed. An entire fleet? No. There was something else at work here...

"Sir," Van Hassell said, "One World News is online for you - they need a statement."

Bleoche shook himself and opened his eyes. This was no dream. He climbed into the hovlim once again, and found the golden-tongued, silver-haired, all-but-fossilised Director General of O.W.N. waiting for him on the screen.

"Well, Mr President sir?", the D.G. asked. He looked stricken.

Bleoche felt old. He felt tired, worn out, just thinking about the colossal, planetary regeneration program that he would be required to instigate, to promote, to co-ordinate, and most wearying of all; to *believe* in. He would also have retaliation, without a doubt. It would come later, but it would make everything worthwhile. When the human race recovered, when they had utterly crushed whoever was responsible for this outrage - he would be triumphant. He would become the most revered and respected leader the world had yet known. See the good, he told himself, see that glorious goal, smell it, taste it, believe it, you have to believe, and then achieving it will come naturally.

He drew a deep breath and said, "The world needs a statement, yes?"

"Yes, Mr President."

"All right, you getting me clearly?"

"Crystal, Mr President."

Bleoche gathered himself into a sombre, austere pose, then began:

"My fellow people of Earth, today we are united in grief for the many, many thousands of innocent human beings who have been brutally murdered by persons or life forms as yet unidentified. The valiant men and women in the emergency services have many weeks and months of serious and horrifying work ahead of them to contain the damage to our cities, and to rescue and heal every person they possibly may. Any citizens wishing to offer help and or medical and food supplies should contact earth.gov, where the appropriate facilities are being set up as we speak."

Van Hassell took note of this with a quick look from Bleoche, and went to see to the creation of the said facilities.

Bloeche continued, "On this black day, while we try to make sense of our loss and our grief, and as we look for those who are to blame, we must remember who we are, and what that means."

He allowed the tears to well up as he spoke.

"We must remember, dear brothers and sisters, that we are human beings. Our spirits shall not be crushed, nor defeated by act of war, nor by act of terror upon our blessed soil, but strengthened by them. Now is the hour in which we bleed, and in which we weep; now is the hour that we are tested, yet now will be the hour that humanity puts aside, once and for all, its differences. One golden day, not too far from now, when we have won as we surely will, history will understand forever that this was our finest hour, for this was the hour that every human being joined together as one great, all-encompassing, almighty force to destroy our deadly foes and emerge as one, glorious, race of heroes and freedom fighters. Make no mistakes, my brothers and sisters, we stand now at the gates of a new age in human history - now will one day be said to have been *the defining moment* in human history."

Unashamed, Bleoche allowed the tear to drop. He bowed his head for a moment, then finished his piece with the words,

"My fellow humans, we are God's children in an uncertain galaxy. Yet we can conquer fear, we can conquer all the odds - He has seen to that. All we need to do, is believe. Oh, my brothers and my sisters; let's make God proud."

He paused, holding the look of sincerity for several seconds, then glanced across the screen at the D.G.

"Was that OK?", he asked.

"Fine," came the reply, "Except you missed out the plugs you're supposed to do."

Bleoche's mouth fell open in surprise. "Now!?", he gasped, his eyes bulging out of their sockets, "You want the plugs as well, NOW, of all times!?"

The D.G. put a hand to his ear, frowning. "They say yes, Mr President. It has to be business as usual."

Bleoche felt his lip curling. "You tell them," he said, in a fierce whisper, "That right now, the world needs a strong hand, a reassuring hand. If I can't give an address such as that, at a time such as this without plugging them and there damned corporate spending economics, the world is not going to unite behind me, nor behind any other corporate puppet they might choose to supplant me. And if they don't like it, tell them they are welcome to try and sue, if they think it will do their publicity any good."

The D.G. looked around himself, nervously. "Listen," he hissed, "You may threaten to damage their popularity with exposures, but they're faceless; anonymous! For God's sake man, remember the Kennedy Alternative!"

"Let them do it!", Bleoche snarled, "I'm the best chance they've got and they know it. Tell them to do whatever they will, but you make sure that little speech of mine gets plenty of airtime. There are far too many witnesses here who saw me give it to you, so its existence can never be denied and therefore you can't be held responsible for letting it out. Then, later on, you can tell *them* to check my popularity ratings, before they make up their minds."

The poor D.G. was stuck 'twixt a rock and a hard place. He put his hand to his ear, fearfully, then relaxed a little.

"They don't like it Mr President sir, but they're prepared to overlook it, this once."

"Damn right they are!", Bleoche exclaimed angrily, and snapped off the link.

Why were corporate executives so dumb? They got away with murder as it was; why were they always pushing the limits?

Bleoche went to look for Van Hassell. He found him busy, speaking with General Kaufman on the vidlink, giving directions for the new facilities to be installed at the earth.gov site. He grabbed Van Hassell by the shoulder, and told him to get the convoy underway again. They were going to join Kaufman in the Octagon, or what remained of the Octagon. He then looked at Kaufman on the link, and told him to have the best four ships from Delta Fleet positioned around Earth to protect her, as soon as they arrived, and the rest were to patrol the solar system in co-ordinated pairs and investigate any unusual readings or activity, with caution.

As he dropped into the comfortable seating of his hovlim for the journey, Bleoche began to calm down. In so doing, he allowed himself to think things through in quiet solitude.

The tumultuous fear began to rise in him then, and he wished he hadn't travelled alone.

***

07/09/2304; 14:23

The whirlwinds were raging around Dr Mary Bleoche. Blood was everywhere. It was all over her white coat and all over the beds. It was spattered on the dull, white walls in many places and it was drenching the rescue workers who were bringing in the injured. The injured were everywhere; coughing, groaning, bleeding and dying. There weren't even a fraction of the doctors and nurses to cope. She toiled ceaselessly, picking the most serious cases to work on, while leaving those not so desperate to the grim duty of waiting, while their very blood was dripping onto the floor.

And the floor was awash. People were slipping in it occasionally, and the constant flow of rescue-workers, helpers, volunteers and the injured, going in and out of the ward, meant that the blood on the floor was constantly being trodden in and around. This liquid was turning more and more filthy with the dirt from peoples shoes.

She was a professional. She had seen blood before. Never this much blood, but she was OK. She kept repeating this to herself as she worked, stitching people up, using regenerative creams on the terrible burns of those who had survived the fires, amputating useless and shattered limbs...

'I'm OK, this is what I was trained for.' And she had to remember that the creams did work on burns; these people would be alright. And she told herself that new limbs would be grown for those who were sent out numb and speechless, staring at the patched up stumps where their arms and legs had once been. She didn't allow herself to think of those who were dying for the want of treatment. She had to try to pick the worst cases, in the hope that the less serious ones would live in the interim. She tried not to notice that most of these cases were not surviving. She was doing her best - she was a professional, she couldn't be responsible for the deaths of everyone - it wasn't her fault that people were dying all around her.

She tried not to think to much about the horror in the people's faces. She answered their questions as best she could. She soon had a system of replies set up, with which most of their desperate pleas could be answered.

"We don't know. I'm sorry, I really am, but no-one has told me who it was or why it happened.", was one.

"I haven't heard the name, no, but I'll get someone to check for you.", was another.

"Meta York was rammed by star ships, that's all I've been told.", was the briefest explanation she could give, and the words, "Just close your eyes, you need rest.", was the best way of dealing with the wild, dying, spluttering frenzy of those for whom she could do nothing.

The best two hospitals in Meta York had been located deep within the bowels of the city, and they must surely have been destroyed when the central spire had come down. She knew she was lucky to have been working in her lab on the outskirts when the disaster happened, but she was scared for the first time since she had separated from her husband. They were dangerously under-equipped. There wasn't enough blood. The remaining banks were empty. Volunteers were being siphoned constantly - she had given two pints herself, small though she was - but the need still outweighed the supply. She hadn't realised how hard she was breathing. She hadn't realised that she was muttering to herself, repeatedly,

"It's everywhere and there isn't enough, it's everywhere and there isn't enough..."

***

07/09/2304; 14:33

In the deepest, darkest sanctuary of the Octagon's underground bunkers, Bleoche was speaking to General Kaufman and the other military chiefs. Van Hassell was present with a consignment of Bodybots assembled around the edges of the room.

"I understand that, General," he said, with infinite patience, "There is no way the crews of Gamma Fleet could have mutinied, nor all turned against Earth. It would be highly unlikely that even one or two potential mutineers could have seen active service for very long. The idea that enough suicidal mutineers existed within the fleet to have taken over every ship and then done this to us, just isn't feasible."

General Kaufman looked distinctly disdainful. He was sitting back in his chair and frowning at the President. His large, resplendent necklace of chins was quivering slightly as it hung over his tight, regulation-standard, bottle-green collar.

"However," Bleoche continued, "The facts are that twenty Class-A space cruisers, each containing over two thousand men, twenty armed escape shuttles and two hundred short-range fighters - twenty of our very finest have just rammed our cities and defences, killing not only themselves but Jesus Christ alone knows how many hundreds of thousands, or even millions more. The world needs answers and it needs them soon; our justice must be swift and merciless."

"Perhaps they weren't actually victorious?", said General Marracha.

"Meaning?", Bleoche asked.

"What I mean to say sir, is that perhaps Gamma Fleet didn't stop the rebellion in the Gondor System. Perhaps they were stopped themselves, imprisoned, brainwashed -"

"Are you suggesting that the minor terrorist rebellion at

Gondor Prime was somehow powerful enough to conquer an entire earth fleet?", Kaufman scoffed.

"No," Marracha replied calmly, "Not in direct conflict, but as you've pointed out, Gamma Fleet was sent to deal with an essentially terrorist group. They may not have faced any standard battles. A terrorist will stop at nothing to make his mark, he will invoke religion to garner the suicidal support of his followers, who in turn will stop at nothing to inflict the greatest damage upon the foe. There must be a million and one possibilities of indirect conflict which we haven't yet considered because they are forbidden by the interplanetary codes of conduct at war."

"Don't we play out every possible scenario in strategic training?", said Bleoche.

The seated military officers all looked at each other.

"Well sir," said Marracha, "Every officer who ascends the ranks is taught about the main attack strategies, the history of conflicts on the ground, on water, in the air, in space and combinations of all four. The history of terrorism is unpredictable, because terrorists don't stick to any one method - they improvise, using secrecy, deception and simplicity in design to wreak the greatest havoc. There are two types of terrorist - the Direction Finders and the Ground Troops. The Direction Finders plan, organise and at higher levels, recruit and brainwash. The Ground Troops are willing to die in any mission they are sent upon, be it suicide bombing or piloting, poisoning, murder sprees, you name it. Few of them ascend any ranks, as most die too soon."

"That did not answer my question.", Bleoche said, sternly.

Marracha seemed highly irritated that the President had noticed.

"There is no real way to plan for terrorist attacks," he said, "That is the whole point of terrorism - maximise the damage and do it where it's least expected. The only way we can combat it is to teach any officers ascending the ranks to think for themselves, to improvise and to do what it takes to overcome the enemy."

Bleoche had his head in his hands. 'Be strong', he told himself, silently.

"Has Delta Fleet been assigned as I ordered?", he asked, raising his head.

"Yes sir, twenty minutes ago.", announced General Kaufman, in grandiose fashion.

"How soon can Alpha Fleet get to the Gondor System?", Bleoche asked.

"A couple of days," said Admiral Hussain.

"Alright," said Bleoche, "This is how we're going to play it: Publicly, the priority must be to save as many lives as possible and spare no expense doing it. We must also assure people that we are protecting them and conducting a thorough and brutally honest investigation into who is responsible for these outrages. Unofficially, the priority is to retrieve the black boxes of as many ships as is possible - we need answers. Also, send Alpha Fleet to the Gondor System.

We aren't going to take this lying down. Make sure that every settlement in the Gondor System knows that Alpha Fleet is on its way, and that they had better surrender any terrorists they're harbouring, or they will suffer the consequences. We must ensure that Alpha Fleet does indeed arrive as promised."

The staff were in general agreement with this, and the meeting was dissolved. Kaufman was left in charge of overseeing the delegation of responsibilities.

***

09/09/2304; 01:07

Dr Mary Bleoche was groggy. She had been working upon the battered, bruised, burned bodies of the stricken and terrified patients for hours uncounted. She had eaten very little, preferring instead the injections of Vita Blast to keep her upright. Still she battled on, borne up by the horror, the blood and the need to stop it flowing away. Her tears were few, and they were under control. She would stay standing as long as the shocked victims were being wheeled through the doors of her ward.

When her favourite nurse, Jacob, saw the state she was in, he demanded that she take a rest. She had been working too long, he told her, and she was obviously on the verge of collapse. She ordered him out, telling him to stop being so silly and tend to people who needed help. He pointed out that she had been working non-stop for over twenty-four hours, hadn't eaten enough food and he also knew about the two pints of blood she had given.

"How many did you give?", she asked him.

He smiled. "Just gave my third," he said, "But I've been eating well to support my habit! You though, you need food *and* rest."

He was a big man, and young. He always wanted to take good care of her, yet he wasn't very good at taking care of himself. Still, he was rather disarming...

Suddenly, his arm was around her. "Come on," he said, "We're going to get you some rest."

She relented, as she often did to Jacob. He was almost young enough to be her son. She often scolded herself for this, but what the hell? It was something in his manner. There were no fairy tales in real life, and if this fresh young specimen wanted to look after the President's first wife this year, there'd always be another next year. Life was too short, anyway.

Jacob supported her with his strong arm as they wandered down the corridor in search of a bed or a couch where she could rest.

"There you are!", said a familiar voice.

The couple turned to see the boss - an accountant-made-good, whose name was Patrick Simms - running down the corridor towards them. He drew up sharply and clutched his pot belly.

"Mary," he cried, "Where have you been? I've been paging you for hours - I thought you'd been killed!"

She answered him in sleepy irritation. "I'm a doctor," she said, "Where the Hell do you think I've been?"

Comprehension lowered Simms' jaw even further. "You've been operating on patients?!", he spluttered.

"Fuck off!", she replied, pointing her finger at him right under his nose, uncaring of consequence, "Some of us took an oath, you know, some of us promised -"

"Stop it Mary!", Simms cried, pushing her hand away.

He then looked at Jacob, "What's she been on?", he asked.

Jacob shrugged.

"Look Mary, we need you at the lab.", said Simms, "You're the expert, and we have a very serious problem which we need you to look into."

"She's been working non-stop for more than thirty-six hours," said Jacob, "She needs a rest."

Simms took this into account. "All right," he said, "Mary, I want to see you in the lab in no more than six hours."

"I've got limbs to sever!", she spat back at him.

"I don't care!", he bellowed in frustration, "You're the best chance we have of getting to the bottom of who or what it was that took over Gamma Fleet! You're the one with the best knowledge of nano-plagues!"

"What?", she said, blinking in surprise, "What about Dr Phillips, or Dr Waterstone, or Professor Bilko?"

"All unreachable," he said, "And presumed dead. It's you we need."

"Come on," said Jacob, "I'll find you a spot to sleep in, and I'll have some food ready for you when you get up."

She looked into his big, brown eyes.

"Oh, OK," she said.

***

09/09/2304; 01:54

Bleoche arrived at his palatial country retreat a very weary man. He had spent the day touring his ruined home city, giving interviews, projecting the image of a man of the people, a brave fighter and noble father figure. He had even done a very televised shift helping the emergency services clear the rubble. He was reasonably strong and healthy for his age, and no public sector worker could claim he hadn't put his back in on the several occasions during his political career in which duty had called him to. Today he had excelled himself, helping to rescue people both dead and alive from the wreckage. This work had been closely watched by the cameras. He had got his hands well and truly dirty, he had worked up a good sweat and shed the necessary tears at the appropriate junctures.

The servants fussed around him like Bodybots and hotel Pimpbots, offering him all manner of refreshments. It made him sick. All he wanted was a quick burger to eat and then a bottle of something very strong.

Later, as he paced the inner sanctum of today's palatial refuge, swigging shamelessly and intermittently from his bottle as he went, he found himself growing angry.

The sheer audacity of it!

One of the six mighty earth fleets, completely taken over and used like monstrous battering rams upon his beloved home planet. The four great defence satellites, Kirk, Picard, Sisko and Janeway; all destroyed. New Vegas, gone. The rubble from the satellites and the star ships which had destroyed them was still in orbit. Sometimes pieces of it would fall flaming, from the skies. Artificial meteors, threatening lives, limbs and planetary harmony for - as the laws of Chaos told him - an indefinite period to follow.

Bleoche went to the window and saw the bright, silver moon. The Earth's Ring (a minor orbital asteroid field, created from the blocks of ice which had been stored there during the Great Warming of two centuries ago) shone brightly; a beautiful silver line across the sky. As he watched, he noticed little flashes lighting up all along the line. Collisions from the orbiting station wreckage, obviously. He realised that he was gripping the window frame too tightly.

"Bad day?"

Bleoche recognised the voice of his eldest (and most legitimate) son, Terry. He didn't turn around.

"What do you think?", he said.

"So, have they any idea yet - I mean, how many?"

Bleoche gripped the window frame even more tightly. "Twenty ships of Gamma Fleet -" he said, in careful monotone, "- Forty thousand people. Some six hundred thousand at New Vegas, nearly fifteen thousand at the four defence satellites and an estimated two million in the various cities, world wide."

"So, no more than three million then?"

Bleoche forced himself to release the window frame and turn to face his son. In the semi-darkness, his face was ugly with venomous intent.

"You've seen the reports," he said, his voice taut, "You know it should be no more than three million."

His flaxen-haired, foppish son breathed a sigh of relief.

"So, it's still far fewer than the number of fatalities which the Earth fleets have inflicted upon the people of Gondor, over the years," the youngster said, "Good! We're still winning!"

Bleoche leapt snarling at his son, and knocked him savagely to the floor.

The President stood glowering over his son. "Get up!", he ordered.

The stricken young man ran his hand over his face to see how much blood there was. Not too much. He breathed deeply in order to control the flood of emotions, then licked his finger clean, and said,

"No thanks Dad. Get yourself a punch bag to take it out on, or why not go and see one of your whores?"

This earned Terry a powerful kick in the ribs. He coughed and spluttered for a few moments, then it turned to giggles and laughter.

"Better still," he wheezed through his chuckling, "Why not kill two birds with one stone and get Mum round here?!"

Bleoche went to beat his son some more, then held back. He was forgetting himself. He smiled down on Terry.

"You know," he said, easily, "That wonderful education we gave you really hasn't taught you anything about life, has it? Every time you start talking this way, you imagine that you're being very perceptive, don't you? Very clever and insightful? You believe that you're saying things which pierce through the armour and make me face things which I'd rather not - don't you?"

"I think your actions speak for themselves," Terry said, quietly.

"Whereas all you're doing, *really* -", Bleoche continued, unabashed, "Is illustrating your own naivety. I think it's about time we had you seen to at Dallas."

That had worked. His son turned very pale. Being the son of an influential senator and later, the son of the President himself, Terry's tirades against what Earth stood for had never really put him in any danger of being sent to the Attitudinal Correction facilities at Dallas. They were usually laughed off, and Terry wasn't daft enough to say these things too often or to the wrong people, for fear of being publicly labelled a 'Detractor'. In reality, Terry had always been fairly safe to say things which would soon have seen anyone else condemned as not just a 'Detractor', but also 'unstable enough to be detained at Dallas for the good of the Realms' until they were deemed 'of suitably-sound mind to re-enter society'.

Bleoche had never threatened his son like this before. He had saved the idea up, mainly because he had had no real need to use it before. After the events of the last two days, things had to be made crystal clear.

No-one who went to the Dallas Institute of Realignment for Earthers ever re-emerged the same. No-one who made it back out to the real world could ever remember their experiences with any clarity, but on coming out again, they were invariably reborn. Where once there existed intolerance, ingratitude and the noxious desire to question authority, policies and regimes; there would be only the desire to fit in, to be loved, and most importantly, anyone re-emerging from Dallas would have the earnest desire to make, and to invest; *money*.

The dark, whispered rumours of what went on at Dallas could never match up to the reality of what it must actually take to change people so utterly. Terry had heard most of the rumours. They were all stories about how, under violent extremes of physical and mental pressure, a person's mind would be opened up, reduced to its component parts and then painstakingly rebuilt in a manner which produced individuals best suited to serve society.

Terry was afraid. He knew that it was well within his father's power to send him to Dallas, he had simply forgotten because it had never been threatened before. However, Earth had never been attacked on such a scale before.

He looked up at his father from where he lay.

"You'd do that?", he said, quavering.

Bleoche scorned the young man with his triumph. "No," he grinned, a sickly sight, "Not unless it's absolutely necessary."

Terry was thinking, quickly. "You know Dad," he said, getting cautiously to his feet, "I know you sent me to the best schools, but -"

"I know that too!", Bleoche cut in, "And if I'd have known what a subversive influence a good education is, you'd never have had one."

"I wasn't going into that, Dad," Terry said, carefully, "I was going to say that even though it was the best school, it still wasn't trouble-free."

Bleoche was growing tired of his son already. "What do you mean?", he said, icily.

"Well, I never told you this at the time, but there used to be this big fat kid with an inflated opinion of himself in my class. His name was Granville. He'd go around every day beating up a lot of the kids and stealing their lunch money. He was never stupid enough to try it on me, obviously, but just about everyone else got it sooner or later."

Bleoche raised an eyebrow. "Never you?"

"With a father like you? Granville wasn't totally stupid. But still, one day it all went wrong. There was this scrawny little kid called David who didn't have many friends, or much money. I think his parents spent just about all they could on keeping him at the school. Granville took what he had, all the same. And then this one day, after Granville's taken what money he had and carried on with his rounds, David pulls a cricket bat from out of nowhere, runs up behind Granville and smashes him around the head with it! And while Granville's unconscious on the floor with a big swollen gash in the side of his head, David goes through his pockets and takes back his money. Only *his* money, mind. Then he looks at all the other kids. He doesn't say a word. He doesn't have to. Every kid who ever lost money to Granville piles in, kicking him while he's down, then they start fighting with each other over the rest of the loot in his pockets."

"Is there a point to that story?", said Bleoche.

"Well, just that, I suppose everyone's the same, inside. Anyway, I've gotta be going."

"Where?"

Terry froze, uncertain. Was his father going to press him about that story?

"I'm going to the Super Mart to get a bottle of wine, then I'm going to see Kim."

"No," said Bleoche, "It isn't safe! Get one of the Bots to fetch it for you."

"What!? I'd rather just go and see what they have."

"What do you mean? The Bots can go for you and relay the footage straight into the computer - you can see exactly what they have by remote! And you can get Kim round here, too."

"No, and no, Dad!"

Bleoche almost smote his son once again, but suddenly the urge wasn't in him anymore.

"Fine," he said, "If you must go out and see her, go out and see her. But why do you need to go shopping?"

"Oh, er, well, you know, 'business as usual' and all that."

"That doesn't explain why you need to go in person," Bleoche countered.

Terry sighed. He didn't want to bring her round here, and he certainly didn't want his father obtaining an inventory of the evening's supplies. It wasn't just that he'd need wine and contraception, there would be other expenses which he could hardly risk running through the main computer. Still, there were any number of nauseating psychological defects - thrown up by their 'Glorious Space Age' - which he could use as cover...

"Look," said Terry, feigning an air of frustration and embarrassment, "I have to *queue*!"

He stormed off, as Bleoche scowled at his fleeing form.

***

09/09/2304; 08:53

Bleoche had only just arrived at the war council, and he found all the military staff waiting for him. His headache was gone, but he was still groggy. After a few quick apologies for being slightly late, he was eager to know what they had been able to find out.

"So come on then," he said, "What can you tell me?"

"It was a nano-plague, sir," said General Kaufman.

Bleoche felt his heart almost stop. He had heard of them, of course, but was hazy on what the exact extent of their capabilities were. He had heard the infamous horror stories of mass swathes of the population of earth being destroyed by them in the past. He knew the general idea - a genetically engineered plague of nanobots would breed in the blood stream and after a certain incubation period, would shred the victims arteries and veins from within, causing a brutally painful death. They were programmed to survive the death of the body, and survive in the air. The worst ones were extremely virulent, and passed on regularly before the death of the victim.

"WHAT!?", cried Bleoche, "So the cities could be infected, as well?"

No-one answered.

"A nano-plague?", he muttered to himself, "Jesus tap-dancing Christ, a goddamn *nano-plague!?*"

"Why weren't the men of the fleet innoculated? I thought every military man had the jabs!"

The assembled militia looked from one to another, uneasily.

"They were, Mr President," Van Hassell whispered in his ear.

"OK," Bleoche said, "What's the worst a nano-plague can do?"

Everyone looked to the man in the corner of the room. Bleoche followed their gaze and his eyes met with a small man, perched on the edge of a chair. His thin, greasy, dark hair was stretched over his shiny pink head, in narrow, slick reams. His puffy cheeks were overshadowed by the bulbous brown eyes, magnified to gigantic proportions by very strong glasses. His lips stood out a little, forming what was almost a beak. He had about his ample figure, a shiny, black leather jacket which creaked slightly as he moved. His arms and legs were unnaturally slim in proportion to the rest of him. The impression he gave to a person seeing him for the first time from a distance, was that of a perversely large beetle.

Colonel Zeetan, MSc, stood up and introduced himself to the President. He was the military expert on biological warfare.

"The most lethal nano-plague ever invented," he said - in the clipped tones of a strange accent which Bleoche couldn't place - "Is a neat little construction named 'The Mincer', by the fleet men, although it's official code-number is 'FKD-

1AD-2BC'. It was developed to cause the maximum damage to the widest possible section of the population. It would never have been contained completely, were it not for two, very important factors. Firstly, it was smart enough not to invade any body which was not human, and secondly, the antidote was cheap and was thoroughly administered to the troops and anyone else who thought they needed it, except of course, the enemy."

Zeetan paused, and sipped from a little glass of water.

"The standard version is a phial of perhaps one million, perhaps ten million nanobots. Each is a microscopic, genetically engineered life form which can enter a persons body painlessly through the pores of the skin. Once they are inside they pass unnoticed into the bloodstream and begin to breed, using blood-cells as food. They are, if you like, micro-vampires. Their breeding follows a specific technique. They are hermaphroditic. They can each recreate with alarming speed. For every ten new nanobots created, three are sent to the lungs to be breathed out into the atmosphere where they may be breathed in by others, and one is sent at random to either the palms of the hands, the lips, the face, neck or genitals, to re-emerge through the pores of the skin and be picked up when in contact with others. The other six

will breed. In this manner they achieve both an exponential expansion within the bloodstream of the victim, and a good chance of infecting others very rapidly."

"How long is the incubation period?", Bleoche demanded.

Zeetan rubbed his lips with his black-gloved hand.

"With 'The Mincer'? Within ten to fourteen days of incubation, the concentration of nanos within the victim's system reaches critical. Then they burrow into the interior wall of every vein and artery, cling on with hooks and begin shredding the vessels wide open. Within seconds the victim's entire arterial system is lacerated. There follows a few moments of agony, as the blood seeps throughout the system and out of every orifice, before death."

"But everyone in the fleets is inoculated," Bleoche replied, so we're dealing with something new, right?"

"Well, yes Mr President," Zeetan answered, "But it's highly unlikely that the design and program of 'The Mincer' could be bettered. Our best scientists have looked to the next advance in genetic technology for a way of bettering it for the larger part of a century, and to no avail. It is generally accepted that we have reached our limits where the technology is concerned, and as every relevant party was long since made privy to the information available, inoculations against the nanos have made them largely redundant."

"Redundant?", Bleoche stared incredulously at the little, black-ensconced man, "REDUNDANT?!?", he screamed at Zeetan, "What the hell happened then? The Gondor system isn't advanced enough to control or understand nanos! How could they have developed something better? Something which kills innoculated men?"

"With respect, Mr President," Zeetan said, looking hurt, "We cannot assume this plague is any better than previous models, it probably just has a very different way of hiding itself from the body's immune systems."

"What the hell?", Bleoche thundered, "Listen, we need everything on this new threat, and we need it yesterday! How the Hell do we know that it hasn't already infected half of the populations of Earth's biggest cities?"

No one answered.

Bleoche clutched his forehead. "I have to inspire people," he muttered to no-one in particular, "I have to tell them we're going to win, we're going to get through this. How can I make myself believe that, when we could already be dead? *I* could already be dead!"

He pointed at Kaufman. "You could, too," he crowed, then he pointed at Marracha and shouted, "You're dead, metal-head! Who're you going to blow up now?!"

"With respect Mr President," said Zeetan, "It's very likely that the nanos were all destroyed when the Gamma Fleet ships were destroyed."

Zeetan looked around him for help. "Didn't they all go up in flames?", he asked no-one in particular.

Bleoche wanted to hit him, but he forced himself to focus.

"Alright," he said, not bothering to try to hide the venom in his voice, "You can stop trying to placate me. We found nanos in the dead bodies, right?"

There was agreement.

"Are they still working?"

No-one spoke.

"Kaufman," Bleoche growled, "The experts who are working on an antidote for this new plague - do they fully understand just how urgent a solution is?"

"I've pulled everyone necessary and many more - we have people working round the clock on it.", he replied.

"Right," said Bleoche, "Keep it quiet too. We don't want a mass panic on our hands."

The generals all looked at each other, nervously.

"Any news on black boxes?", Bleoche asked.

"Not yet, Mr President.", said General Heinz, "But it's safe to assume that the crews of Gamma Fleet were hit by the plague, died, then suicide squads boarded the cruisers in order to pilot them into the targets.

Alright," said Bleoche, "But we still haven't established how the Gondor rebels obtained nano-technology. Anyone?"

The officers around the room looked at each other. Some shifted in their seats, uncomfortably.

"Well?!", Beloche demanded.

Kaufman spoke, white-faced. "Well sir, there were some reports a couple of months ago, of elements in the Gondor

System exchanging supplies with the governing bodies of Elsinore System."

Bleoche looked around blankly for an explanation.

This time it was General Marracha who answered. "Elsinore is the nearest system to Gondor sir, and we have had... dealings with Elsinore for many decades."

"Dealings? What *dealings*?" They were keeping something from him - all of them were, he could tell. The officers around the table were all shuffling in their seats and looking sideways, furtively, to see if anyone else would grasp the nettle. A dozen or more multi-chins hung in wobbling shame over shiny collections of medals which ranged in quality from the quite impressive, to the spectacular.

"DAMMIT!", Bleoche screamed at them, "Do any of you want to win this war?!"

There were nods all round, though the furtiveness remained, as did the uncomfortable silence.

"Then tell me; what is it that I need to know?"

Marracha cleared his throat, then said, "Well sir, the governing bodies of Elsinore Prime had trouble for many years with their own rebels, as you know."

"Yeah," Bleoche said, "We moved in with the artillery and helped them wipe out the rebellion - or that's how the history tells it. What are *you* telling me?"

Marracha looked around for help but found all eyes cast

down. He sighed, then said, "We helped them quash the rebellion with controlled nano-plagues, sir."

Bleoche was dumbstruck. "Nanos? Why wasn't this information made available to me before?"

"Why do you think?", Marracha replied, "Your predecessor could hardly let it be known that he had given away the secrets of so dangerous and deadly a weapon in return for mining and property assets."

Bleoche shook his head.

The silence around him bit into his psyche and he couldn't take it anymore. Without warning he exploded, unleashing the torrent of abuse which had been building up in him for the last few days. His predecessor's ancestry was brought into a hideously foul and incestuous disrepute, and everyone else in the room was befouled with the most colourful and vigorously spiteful language, not to mention a multitude of the most randomly-grotesque, physical and sexual metaphors which his red-blooded fury could muster. He also ensured everyone knew that, as accessories to these outrageous actions, they could all be facing utter ruin by the time he'd finished with them.

The atmosphere was electric, yet almost static. It seemed everyone was holding their breath. Barely even an eye flickered out of place.

After the longest silence yet, Bleoche knew he would have to give up his brooding.

"How far away from Gondor System is Alpha Fleet?", he

asked, wearily.

"They should be there within two hours," said Admiral Hussain.

"Good," said Bleoche, "I want those planets scoured. I want anything which looks suspicious from orbit, destroyed. No-one is to land, nor set foot on the planets though - we don't want them being at risk of the nano-plague, but the whole of Gondor is going to pay for this. Do I make myself clear?"

"Yes Mr President," came the many hurried, thankful replies.

"I also want them to understand that under no circumstances will any of them survive if anything like this ever befalls us again. They have to be beaten and scared into utter submission; we will not tolerate systems which harbour terrorists or which allow them to hide within their borders."

Kaufman spoke for all when he said, "Consider it done, Mr President."

***

10/09/2304; 11:46

Cut to a TVNet screen; Channel 12480. It's a daytime discussion show for celebrities, politicians, journalists and commentators.

Humphrey Dimpleton, the show's venerable host and co-ordinator was speaking. "We now have a question from Mrs Hillary West," he said, "A housewife from Indianapolis, who wants to know 'How does President Bleoche keep up his strength and his spirits so well?'"

Before anyone else could say anything, the comedian on the panel of four - Thomas Marks - got the audience laughing by making the hand-gesture for opiates.

"Yes," said Dimpleton, smiling, "Yes, thank you Mr Marks! Josephine, you're acquainted with the President; any thoughts?"

Josephine Orange was a tall, elegant, proud woman, whose barely tamed mass of wild, dark hair made her seem younger than her forty-three years. Her political career had not advanced as far as it might have done by now, as she had found her opinions made her more money in the media than they would have done in the higher echelons of power. These higher echelons were also dangerously reptilian and extremely restrictive. She had begun to understand, many years ago, that her influence could be far better spread to the people via the TVNet and its subsidiaries.

"I think President Bleoche is simply a very brave and strong man," she said, earnestly, "And he wouldn't be where he is if he wasn't so strong. I think he understands that he has to be stronger than ever to fight this new threat and of course, to inspire us to come together and do what has to be done. I mean really, he has no choice in the matter - it's do or die."

There was massive applause. You never knew, just from watching a show online, whether the applause was spontaneous or induced.

Before the applause had died down, Roger Waiter had to start speaking. He was a writer, journalist and amateur philosopher; a slim, middle-aged man with wispy, thinning hair. This was unusual. He knew that this appearance belittled him before people of dubious intellect, for why would he not simply have his hair replaced like every other baldy did?

"You know," he announced over the fading din, "You know that Bleoche will also be taking this attack very personally, and he's never been one to back out of a fight."

"I tried to start a fight with him once," said Thomas Marks, "I woke up in intensive care!"

More laughter, and some cheering.

"The important thing isn't whether or not we'll win," said Roger Waiter, "Of course we'll win, but where will Bleoche take us afterwards? I mean, terrorism is a symptom endemic in conquered populations, and I think we have to ask whether or not we should look at better communications and commerce with the Gondor System."

The moment of total silence was swiftly broken by Josephine Orange.

"I believe," she said, frostily, "That in the light of these outrageous attacks upon our planet, any system which encourages, supplies or harbours terrorists should be brought directly to account. It's them who should be afraid!"

There was a general cheer and huge applause, beckoned on and strengthened by Orange herself. Sensing trouble, Waiter leaned back in his chair and prepared himself to hold his tongue on the subject.

"In fact -", Orange continued speaking with due seriousness, directly to the audience, "It's about time we had a little bit of respect from some of these systems!"

More applause. She knew exactly where she was taking them, and Waiter knew it too. He felt the cold sweat begin to dampen his skin. The colour was draining steadily from his features.

"We have given these alien species gifts they couldn't even have imagined before they met us! We've brought them culture; mass entertainment, thriving media services, cities and industry! Every new form of intelligence we come across seems to be living together like worms before we show them what they're capable of!"

Applause, cheering; Roger Waiter clutched his brow.

"Who brings civilisation to the Galaxy?", Orange cried, exuberantly, "Come on, who?"

"We do!", "Us!" and "Humans!", came the leering, uncoordinated replies from the audience.

"We give these other misguided races the gift of Capitalism, we gain valuable assets in return and all you can do (she pointed an accusing finger at Waiter) is moan and whinge about it!"

She turned to the crowd. "What is he?", she asked them, knowing already that they would give the right response.

"Detractor!", they all yelled back.

The chanting began, "DE-TRAC-TOR!... DE-TRAC-TOR!... DE-TRAC-TOR!", along with the furious waving of pointed fingers in Roger Waiter's direction.

Roger Waiter stood up with quiet dignity, and was booed and hissed off the stage.

"Now then," Humphrey Dimpleton began, raising his hands to try to calm the audience down, "Now then, let's settle down a little, we've still got half a show to get through!"

He winked at Josephine Orange. "They're well trained, aren't they?", he said, quietly enough for the restless audience not to hear him. Orange smiled knowingly at him.

"Mr Lydon," Dimpleton said to the fourth panel member, who had been quiet for most of the show, "What do you predict for the future?"

Stuart Edward Lydon was a producer of films and TVNet broadcasts and interactive services. It was this fact which prompted Thomas Marks to cut in once again with;

"Hundreds of new war films and documentaries - and lots of enormous pay cheques!"

Lydon had been brooding for some time, but now he joined in with the friendly laughter.

"Well -" he began, but it's getting boring, so let's flip the channel...

10/09/2304; 11:51

Channel INFO-24/7; the News. This is the only channel to rival One World News in its global influence. This quarter's newscaster, Chastity Sayer, is speaking. She's a perfectly-formed, three-dimensional, youthful-looking, digitised woman with fantastically-proportioned curves, barely contained in colourful, skin-tight garb. She has deep, green eyes and an enticing, short, mahogany haircut atop an incredibly pretty, angular face.

"In the new war on terrorism, Earth's Alpha Fleet has arrived at the Gondor System and is currently demolishing all asteroids orbiting their sun. This is in an attempt to weed out the terrorists who clearly survived Gamma Fleet's recent purge. Many suspected terrorist strongholds upon the surface of Gondor Prime, Gondor Gardens and Gondor Graveyard have also been raided. Official sources say that CSPs were kept to a reasonable minimum. The native Gondorians have been given just two hours to hand over all remaining terrorists, before suffering the consequences of harbouring intergalactic criminals and perpetrators of genocide..."

Ah, sweet Chastity! It was often viewed as a shame that such glorious works of art were always discarded for a new model within three months. The trouble with having such sexy presenters who never grew older, was that dispite their potential immortality, they could never be allowed to remain as presenters for too long. Hackers would invariably use their know-how to simulate a near-perfect match of each new newscaster, to be placed directly into the most graphic, disgusting, porno-footage imaginable. Within three months, the male population would usually be voting the new virtuagirl into a top ten place on the weekly 'World's Sexiest Woman' polls, but more importantly, the planetary communication systems would also be jammed with file-clips of the channel's star newscaster in the most explicit and believably-vile positions imaginable - all in eager transit from one leering voyeur to the next. This situation was perhaps to be expected, but there was a limit to the denigration and degradation which any newscaster could suffer before she became unfit to make the news serious and believable.

***

11/09/2304; 07:10

Bleoche was tired beyond belief. Tired of having to present a relentlessly indomitable spirit to the cameras, tired of having to weep for the dead in public, tired of the endless questions about the future from uncertain civil servants, civilians, and worst of all; reporters. He had fallen asleep in his hovlim as it took him back to the Octagon for the daily meeting with his chiefs of staff.

It was the alarm which woke him. It seeped into the firestorms of his subconscious mindscape, a growing warning. He awoke with a start. There was a message waiting for him. He flicked on the TVNet system and opened it.

"Mr President," General Kaufman's pixelised image said,

gravely, "We have good news. We have our first black box sir - and it's from the *Enterprise*."

***

11/09/2304; 07:37

On Bleoche's entry, the atmosphere in the conference chamber was like death. Bleoche looked around him, grittted his teeth and decided to give them the benefit of the doubt.

"So what does the black box tell us?", he asked.

"We've yet to view the captain's log," said Kaufman, "But according to the onboard crew monitor, everyone on the *Enterprise* died at almost exactly the same moment, some two days before reaching Earth."

"Everyone? *At the same time?*"

Bleoche was getting that sick feeling once again. It was becoming familiar to him, and that was the most sickening feeling of all.

"I thought nano-plagues only had a ninety to ninety-five percent efficiency? And how the hell can they all have gone at the same time?!"

The generals looked at each other. "This appears to be a new strain," said Colonel Zeetan, quietly.

"Possibly set off by some signal," Kaufman said, "Perhaps by... A radio transmission, or -"

Bleoche rounded on him. "You fucking arsehole!", he screamed, "The next time you tell me you've got good news, you'd better damn well mean it!"

"Sir, I -"

"Sir, you *nothing!*" Bleoche spat at him, "Have Delta Fleet scour our system, top to bottom - all scanning methods, all planets, moons -"

"It's underway already sir," Kaufman said.

"Where's the likeliest place for any intruders to hide?"

General Stokes spoke, "The asteroid belt, sir."

Bleoche noticed several of the men giving Stokes poisonous looks at this.

"What's the problem gentlemen?" he asked them, "Do you disagree with General Stokes' interpretation?"

Heads turned, eyes were caught; all judging where the safest course lay, looking for direction.

"Sir they're unhappy because while I'm right, if you take the necessary course of action and order the asteroid belt disintegrated, many valuable mining opportunities would be destroyed as well."

Stokes spoke heavily, his large, frowning, craggy brow threatening to smother his eyes.

Bleoche considered. "Why are you right?" he said.

"Because the moons and planets are easier to scan, even those with cave systems, whereas the asteroids are relatively large in number and very well spread out. Also, if a terrorist were caught by an Earth cruiser on or under the surface of a moon not facing the Earth, he'd have far less chance of reaching a place where he could send the killer signal. On an asteroid, he'd have a far better chance."

Bleoche looked around him. "What are the chances?" he asked, "Are people infected?"

"We've taken samples from the wounded," Colonel Zeetan said, "And there *is* a danger."

"Right," said Bleoche, "Destroy the asteroid belt. Make sure Delta Fleet makes this a priority."

The crescendo of protest which broke out around him was something of a surprise. His staff were vastly opposed to the wholesale destruction of the solar system's asteroid belt, not only because of the mining opportunities which existed for now or for future generations, but also for the loss of heritage.

"The order stands!" Bleoche roared, "*Right now* is what's important, and right now we've suffered enough. I'm not taking any chances."

There followed a sulky, subdued silence, which only made Bleoche more angry.

Zeetan spoke, "Shouldn't we warn people?" he asked.

"Are you mad?" Bleoche said, turning to General Marracha.

"How's the antidote coming?"

"We're told it will be ready in time," came the reply, "Don't panic."

"Panic?", Bleoche said, incredulously, "Panic? Why would I panic? I'm surrounded by men who command a series of mammoth star fleets which have conquered all the systems local to Earth! We are feared and respected for light years in every direction, until one of our own fleets is infected with the most devastating nano-plague ever invented, taken over and used as battering rams against us!"

Bleoche pounded the table with his fist, sending his coffee mug skidding across the table, where it plopped onto Colonel Zeetan's lap.

"The finest intergalactic fighting force known to man!", Bleoche thundered, his brow creased tightly, his eyes manic, "With the best fighters, the best intelligence... WHERE WAS THE FUCKING INTELLIGENCE?!", he screamed.

Everyone was deathly still and silent, which made it all the more difficult for Colonel Zeetan. He was trying feebly to mop his lap before too much coffee soaked in and made it look as though he'd wet himself, but he didn't want to be the only one in the room moving.

It isn't the red colour of the cloth which makes the bull charge, it's the *movement*...

"How was this plague created?", Bleoche continued, "Did no-one think to keep a very close watch on Elsinore, after your secret little trade-off?"

"Our resources have always been a little thinly spread," said Admiral Hussain, "And the Elsinore system has been stable since the old rebellion was crushed."

As Bleoche turned upon Hussein, the full force of the tornado flashing in his eye, Zeetan made a flurry of little movements to mop his lap properly.

"Someone's going to get thinly fucking spread before this is over," Bleoche hissed, dangerously, "Does anyone want to draw straws?"

There was a silence, and Bleoche said, "I want to speak to the people working on the innoculations."

"I assure you sir," said Kaufman, "These people understand the dangers and they will not stop working on the problem until they've solved it."

"What if they don't solve it in time?"

"With respect sir, we still have six days," said General Heinz, "And we've been assured it will take no more than three."

"That's cutting it fine!", Bleoche fired back, "We'll need to innoculate the whole damn planet! And what's more - how do you know we've got six days? We've been outmanoeuvred by this plague on every other front, haven't we?"

Again, silence.

Bleoche threw his hands up into the air. "Right!", he cried,

"Whatever." He sat down, and said nothing.

"Might I suggest that we see what Captain Shamim had to say in his logs?", General Stokes asked. Stokes was a quiet man generally, but he was ever the logician.

"It doesn't seem there's much else we can do," he continued, "We still don't know how the ships were infected, nor how they were controlled, once the crews were dead."

Everyone suddenly found a voice with which to agree.

The doomed Captain Shamim was a reasonably competent soldier with perfectly built, square shoulders and a firmly chiselled face; the face of a hero. This was a visage which would look assured and powerful on any TVNet broadcast.

His first few entries were routine. This big, powerful, patriotic man had recorded various events of no relevance to his mission; a fracas between some of his men - for which they were given two weeks of menial duties, a few minor fluctuations in the *Enterprise's* power matrix and at one point on the outward journey, the *Hood* temporarily lost her hyperdrive capabilities, causing the rest of the fleet to wait for her for more than an hour.

The Gondorians were a lizard-like people, greenish-brown in hue. They moved upon four of their six limbs, or two when hurrying. Their eyes were yellow, with vertical, black slits for pupils. Communications with them were, at best, difficult. They had totally different vocal emissions which sounded like a mixture of whining and hissing. Most communication with them was done via computers which helped translate dialogue, and sometimes with the aid of a couple of qualified translators.

The Enterprise had two such assistants for their talks with the Gondorians. On arrival at Gondor Prime, the fourth planet of the system, the governing bodies of the planet were united in offering the fleet any supplies or shore-leave which they might require. They seemed eager to appease the Captain of the Earth fleet, yet all their offers were politely turned down by Captain Shamim, except for the offer of information.

A contingency of governors and military leaders from Gondor Prime had travelled into orbit, that they might liaise with Captain Shamim and some of the other captains of Gamma Fleet.

"That must be it!" said Kaufman, "They passed it on to the captains, who passed it on down to their men!"

"Only five of the captains were at the liaison," said Stokes, tightly, "How could it have got onto the other fifteen ships?"

"I've always said there's something of the 'detractor' mentality in you, Stokes," Kaufman retorted.

"Don't start!" Bleoche told them, "We need to *know*, not guess."

The President and his top-brass military men in the dimly-lit conference room, followed Captain Shamim's visual log through the meeting, all of which was conducted with the utmost precautionary measures in place. The Gondorians were conveyed to the secure meeting room without meeting a single human, nor passing through any of the crew's areas. The 'Secure-Confer' additions had been made standard onboard every earth ship many decades before - following several notorious assassinations and biological attacks.

The meeting room was a focal point at which up to twenty-five people or known, sentient life-forms could meet and confer, yet remain totally, physically, isolated from each other in the twenty-five separate, self-contained booths. A delegation could arrive on board, attend a conference and leave without ever entering the same environment as that in which the human crew lived.

Watching the footage, Bleoche and his men became satisfied that the Gondor contingency was not responsible, or at least, not directly responsible for the fate of Gamma Fleet. Not only had the 'Secure-Confer' protocols been strictly observed, but every one of the Gondorians had remained in their bio-suits, the entire time they were onboard the *Enterprise*. Shamim was an experienced officer, who took no chances where rebellions were concerned. He knew from early experiences that not only were biological weapons extremely easy for terrorists to use, but that you could never be sure (until it was too late) who the terrorists were.

The meeting had revealed that the Gondorians had good intelligence to indicate that the rebellion had fled Gondor Prime in a small fleet of space ships and were hiding in the asteroid belt between the second and third planets of the system, occasionally making raids for supplies upon the farms of the third planet (Gondor Gardens) and the mines of the second (named Gondor Graveyard because of its barren, almost inhospitable landscape).

Shamim had politely asked the delegates why had not been able to deal with the rebellion.

The Gondorians skulked, mewed and hissed nervously, before telling the Captain that they had sent a unit of police ships to control them, but had been defeated by the ferocity and cunning of the rebels - and by the defection of half of the police squad to the terrorist ranks.

Captain Shamim was very much less than impressed. "These wretched, fucking lizards" were so inept at controlling their own people, that an attempt to police the rebels had succeeded only in making them stronger. These remarks were translated back to the Gondorian delegation, minus the abundant curses.

At this observation, the Gondorians had whined that they needed more help - most of their populations were sick of Earth and its demands.

Shamim told them to do better, and reminded them that their status as heads of state gave them extremely favourable returns from the Gondor-Earth Trade System. It would be a shame to have to install new leaders, he told them, and took care to remind them what this alternative would mean for them, their people and their planet.

The Gondorians left the *Enterprise* in a very subdued manner.

After the meeting, Shamim's mission had been simple. Gamma Fleet set sail for the asteroid belt, and spent a month systematically annihilating it. Some of the rebels were lost in the destruction, some gathered to fight back, and some ran for Gondor Gardens or Gondor Graveyard. Gondor Prime was out of range on the other side of the system at the time.

Those who stood their ground were slowly penned in by Gamma Fleet and its hordes of fighters. A few of the fighters were destroyed, but the rebels were completely overwhelmed. Their ships were inferior; their weapons couldn't penetrate the massive Gamma Fleet cruisers' shielding. When their weapons were all spent, Gamma Fleet didn't instantly destroy them. The rebels' ships were punctured, one by one, so their atmospheres drained out of them, slowly. The rebels had plenty of time to try to escape the inevitable, yet they were mercilessly held back at every point. Their cries for help were jammed at the source; no other Gondorians would ever hear them.

Within two hours they were all lifeless, except for one. One indomitable troop of spacers actually managed to plug the holes in their ship and restart their engine. It took them over an hour and a half, during which time the scans indicated that half the crew had died and the rest were brushing with death on a knife-edge, yet somehow they managed to save themselves. All the while, Gamma Fleet hung silently in space, waiting. Then, as soon as the survivors of this pathetic little ship had saved themselves, the *Enterprise* had punctured their ship again. It took little more than fifteen minutes to finish them off, this time.

Bleoche and his war council were satisfied with this, and with Captain Shamim's pursuit of the others who had fled. These runaways had disappeared into the oceans of Gondor Gardens or into the mines and caves of Gondor Graveyard. A leisurely carpet-bombing of the relevant areas had ensured an extremely minimal chance of survival for all the remaining rebels.

Not particularly dwelt upon at this meeting, was the number of Gondorian civilians who must also have perished in the bombings. These were the miners who toiled endlessly in the EarthCore-run Plutonium Pits of Gondor Graveyard, and the farmers and fishers of Gondor Gardens, whose efforts helped feed both Earth's population and the Gondorian bourgeoisie.

In addition to these CSPs ('conflict-superfluous purges', as they were officially referred to), there were many transport ships in the wrong areas at the wrong moments which were also destroyed, simply for the fact that they were spaceships, and therefore not easily distinguishable from rebel spaceships.

The war council were at a loss. They could find no fault with any of Shamim's actions - he had acted with total awareness of all conceivable dangers, and with proper, military precision in dealing with those who opposed Earth and its interests. There were no gaps in his game plan. After the successful erasing of all undesirable elements, Gamma Fleet had dropped almost twenty-thousand supply bundles down to the Gondorians in the affected areas of the two planets, passed a none-too subtle warning message on to the authorities of Gondor Prime, and left the system.

Once Gamma Fleet had left the system, Captain Shamim had finished off his logs on the mission with all final reports and statistics, followed by a short concluding speech;

"Once again," he spoke into the imager, "It has been an honour for me and for all my men to serve 'that good 'ol sapphire globe'*. All the men have performed to the best of their abilities, and I hereby recommend the following for top-level commendation."

There followed a list of some eleven or twelve Captains and Lieutenants, before Shamim closed off, saying;

"...And now we return home, maximum speed. That is all."

The rest of the information which the black box had recorded, was just routine systems reports, flight path and life-signs of the crew. All these life signs had expired within sixty seconds of each other, two weeks after Captain Shamim's last entry.

Within an hour of this, there was an non-sanctioned docking. Three Gondorian life-signs had boarded the *Enterprise*, and two days later was the devastation of September seventh.

"God damn it!" Bleoche yelled, "There's nothing! No indications! How did it happen?!?"

---

* Taken from the chorus of the anthemic 'One Heart, One Home', a favourite old pop-rock song amongst Spacers;

"And if the hands of fate should break me,
Don't leave me cold, please don't forsake me,
Bring me back to that good 'ol sapphire globe,
Source of my light, my heart; my home,"

"We're just as much in the dark as you are, Mr President," Van Hassell murmured in his ear, "And at the moment, the important thing is that the world needs another statement - One World News just buzzed me."

"Fine," Bleoche said, "I'll just have to leave the detective work to you genii."

He stood up and looked around the room at his war staff. "Get me some answers, gentlemen," he told them.

He left the room and marched down the dim, grey corridor. His teeth were grinding. He was whispering vehemently to himself, making promises about the changes he was going to forge in this organisation.

He had not yet reached the nearest private vidscreen, when his wife buzzed him.

He knew immediately that it was her - the familiar old chiming within his mind was, without a doubt, her unique tone.

Bleoche was surprised. While most people handed out their codes to anyone they chose, only a handful of people on earth were allowed access to inter-cranial contact with their President. He had never got around to removing her name from that privileged list, yet they hadn't spoken in the two years since Terry's graduation. What could she want?

Intrigued, Bleoche touched his ear and she connected.

"Antoine," her delicate voice sounded beautifully in his ears, "I need to speak to you about the nano-plague."

"Hello Mary, how are you?" he said, "What do you know the nano-plague?"

"Chivers assigned me to the case, I had no choice."

"Ah, right," Bleoche said, "And you'd rather have been tending the injured and saving lives, yes?"

"Don't start, Ant," she said, "This is important. I know how the nanos were so successful."

Bleoche stopped walking.

"Go on," he said.

"Ant, they can eat through metal."

"What!?"

"It's true," she said, "They latch onto metal and they *eat* it. By doing this, they can bore holes through metal of any thickness. I couldn't believe it myself until we worked out why our samples kept reducing in number - they were eating through the glass of the petri dishes, then going through the metal and plastics in the lab and its furniture."

"Wait a minute," said Bleoche, "How is that possible? Are you saying they can eat through a ship's *hull*? That can't be right - in outer space, that'd blow a ship wide open!"

"No Ant, that's the really clever part - they can pass the atoms through their bodies and reassemble their physical structure as part of a greater whole behind them as they go - there isn't any material we have which can contain them."

Bleoche lost his temper again. Mary listened patiently as he wore out his extensive vocabulary of expletives, before saying,

"Ant, we can stop it - we're close to developing the anti-nanos right now - but this is by far the most destructive nano-plague ever invented. I don't know how long it will be before they reach critical mass - you need to come in and have your blood siphoned through a dialysis machine."

"What?"

"It's the only quick way of making sure you stay alive, even if there are more casualties."

Bleoche found himself smiling, his eyes were wide. "You still care," he murmured.

"A president like you is the only thing that can hold us together and bring us through this," she countered, "It's the good of us all I'm concerned about."

"Whatever," he said, "But don't worry - it's not a 'critical mass' design - it's triggered by a radio signal, and Delta Fleet is currently securing the entire system. If anyone out there is going to try it on Earth like they did with Gamma Fleet, they won't stand a chance."

"Ant, come to me now! It won't take long, then I'll leave you alone."

"Give me an hour," he told her, "I've a broadcast to do that won't wait."

"Still a slave to it all, then?"

"You've seen the news," he replied, then he decided to change the direction, "If I do come to see you today, what will you do if I don't leave *you* alone?"

She hesitated - and that was enough for him. He knew what to do and say when they met once more.

"We've had this conversation a thousand times, Ant," she said, "And every time it ends the same way."

"Yes, you're right," he said, "But every time it happens, isn't it always fun while it lasts?"

He disconnected before she could reply.

***

11/09/2304; 07:00

Motionless upon a dark asteroid the small, metal ship sat waiting in the shadows. Its hull had a thick, well-constructed, matt finish to confuse scans and prevent the reflection of light. The asteroid drifted slowly amongst the scattered field, revolving gently.

The shock waves were growing steadily closer. Delta Fleet's systematic annihilation of asteroids was encroaching upon the dormant ship.

Within the stationary vessel, its pilot and co-pilot - the Gondorians, Biberkay and Hotay - were equally motionless in the darkness. As the debris from the destruction began to cascade past their ship, Hotay could stand it no longer.

"We must move now!" he hissed through the blackness.

"I am quite clear," replied Biberkay, "On the last orbit's viewings and readings, I am assured we have another of the vermin's *hours* before we need to leave. Even the slightest measure of time counts, as you know well. Or were you perhaps aspiring to survive our little venture?"

Hotay was silent.

"Do not forget," the pilot continued, "Another of these hours could mean another two hundred thousand fatalities! Our two lives are worth the statement on behalf of the Holy Crusade, as the ancient prophecies foretold."

"Yes Biber," said Hotay.

"Consider the fifty-three brothers and sisters which our cause has already devoted to the glorious Initial Strike, not to mention the countless atrocities we have suffered with the continued slaughter of our people, the blatant lies, the thieving of our resources and our culture! Would not the Almighty Zesparoth herself shower we two with the full spread of our greatest hopes and dreams, upon entering Her realms after such noble sacrifices?"

"I can see her now," said Hotay, his scales beginning to glow in the deep dark.

"Cease this light!" Biberkay ordered in indignation, "And do not allow visions of Our Saviour to thus engorge thine emotions. Blasphemy remains an offence, even for a martyr."

"'Twas not the Almighty of whom I spoke," claimed Hotay, "'Twas of the peasant girl I would have her grant me!"

Biberkay twitched his annoyance into a drumming rebuke upon the metal wall, after which the two resumed their meditative silence. The onboard proximity detectors were not one hundred percent accurate, but they were consistent in their irregularity and they supported Biberkay's interpretation of the situation.

On the waiting went. The tension Hotay was feeling felt as if it would shred his soul. This was his final hour, after which would come the horror of death followed by the beauty of sweet salvation and then untold glories in the world beyond.

The rumbles of shock waves were becoming noticeable before Biberkay ordered their evacuation of the hiding hole.

"How long do we have?" Hotay wanted to know.

"Once clear, they'll finish us very quickly," Biberkay replied, "And they're already jamming all frequencies as a precaution."

"Will the explosion be enough to penetrate the jamming?"

Biberkay's gills rustled. "Enough. Yes; enough." he said, "Only humans could develop such a hideous weapon as radiation, yet only we have the courage to use it for a simple communication. Yet first - make sure it is set properly."

Hotay inspected his instruments and then reported, "All parameters optimal."

Biberkay flexed his derma and took the controls. "In the gloried name of the Almighty Holy Mother," he intoned, with Hotay joining the recitation midway,

"We shall all be set free."

He gripped the controls, zapped full power through the dormant systems and reared the vessel off the asteroid.

***

11/09/2304; 08:00

Aboard Delta 7, the *Indefatigable*, Monitoring Lieutenant Gatz witnessed the launch of the speedy, highly manoeuvrable ship, from his station and yelled out to his Captain,

"Sir, we've got a ship! Minus two, seven-point-five, thirty-nine, bearing dead away from us!"

Captain Buchannan's balled fists were planted fiercely upon his hips as he strode up and down his bridge, overseeing the systematic annihilation of the asteroid field. At this information from Lieutenant Gatz, he punched the air and shouted in jubilation. The kill would be his!

"Bring it on screen," he ordered, "Commander Duvall!"

"Sir!" said the Comms Officer,

"Are you certain we're jamming all possible channels?"

"Yessir!"

"Good. Commander Manson!"

"Sir!" said the Weapons Officer,

Captain Buchannan's lip curled slightly as he saw the little ship on the viewer speeding away from them, and he said,

"Turn that ship inside out."

"Yessir!"

The bolts of light which flew out from the vast flanks of the *Indefatigable* laced through the little ship from Gondor instantly, and the explosion which followed lit the bridge of the *Indefatigable* as it had never been lit before. The entire cruiser was slightly shaken by the force of the blast.

After shaking his head and rubbing his eyes to try to erase the blinding flash which had stained his retinas, Captain Buchannan peered at the scattered, glowing remains of the ship and said,

"What the hell was that?"

"Radiation sir," Gatz said, "They must have rigged a goddamn nuke to their own hyperdrive!"

Buchannan stared at the darkening fragments on the viewer. "Why?" he said, "They must have known that couldn't harm us - not with our shields up!"

He looked around his crew, askance.

The Comms Officer was the only one to realise the possible reason for the Gondorian rebels last, lunatic gesture of defiance. He had heard a strange screaming across the jammed channels, the moment the explosion happened. Now, he was white as a sheet...

***

11/09/2304; 07:30

Terry and Kim had risen early for sex and were now lying in each others arms, another happy forty-five minutes before they'd need to get up and join the wreckage removal teams.

"I can't believe you actually liked my poetry," she said, "I didn't think you were into stuff like that."

"Well that just goes to show you don't know everything about me, doesn't it?"

He stroked her neck with one hand and teased her in gentle intimacy with the other.

"Mmmm," she murmured, "What do you like about it?"

"There's just such a startling purity to it," he said, "It's almost divine."

That stopped her in her tracks, and she let out an involuntary squeal of surprise. "Me?", she said, in astonishment, *"Pure?!"*

He laughed.

"Physical purity is only ever one shower away babe, or if

you're unlucky; that and a course of treatment. I'm talking about the purity of the emotions in your writing. I mean, you seem to invoke the movements, growth and survival of all the flowers and fruits of an entire Garden of Eden into a poetical image of either perfect understanding, total horror, absolute ecstasy, complete loss, or pure love - pure emotion. That's what makes it so beautiful. It's brilliant."

Kim looked at Terry, wide-eyed. Her mouth was slightly open.

"Wanna shag?", she asked.

They certainly had time, he decided.

Terry seized Kim and they began wrestling with each other, grinding their bodies together urgently as they fought, kissed and bit each other in the struggle for supremacy. Kim was losing so she resorted to tickling him, knowing he couldn't stand it. He let go of her, yelping, but she carried on. Terry gritted his teeth, grabbed her again and pushed himself on top. He forced her hands up behind her head, pinning her down. She struggled against him for a few seconds, then started giggling.

"That makes you *so* easy!" she said, "It's too much fun - I'm going to have to keep doing it!"

Terry grunted and shook her wrists. "Then I'm going to have to keep overpowering you and pinning you down," he said, darkly.

For the first time, she showed him a look of fear, then said

"Good!"

Their lovemaking had barely begun, when Terry heard that familiar chime within his head. In horror, he stopped his motion and looked around in desperation. He could ignore it, but the call had already ruined things.

"What's wrong?" Kim urged, still caught in the heat of the moment.

"Oh Jesus, God, NO!" Terry cried, "How do you always *know*, you bitch?!?"

Kim broke up into giggles, as Terry's passion physically receded and slipped out of her in defeat. He rolled over into his own space, flipped his earpiece with involuntary disgust and said,

"Mum, this is *NOT* a good time."

Now, as if the defeat were not complete enough in itself, his mother was laughing at him as well.

"Like that, is it!" Dr Mary Bleoche said to her first born, "Well I hope I didn't spoil Kim's pleasure for the whole day!"

"Oh, for fuck's sake, mum! Something here is just not fucking right!"

"You can ignore my calls, if you want to!" she reminded him.

Terry looked into Kim's eyes, and knew that his mother

understood the catch she had on him.

"No I can't," he said, "It's either cut off this channel or have you agree to call me *only* in working hours, which I thought you'd already promised me that you'd do."

"Oh, dear me," she said, "Is it *always* so important?"

Terry ground his jaw. Did he really have to put up with this? Had his parents had to put up with such invasions on such a scale, in their day?

"You sound like Dad," he replied.

Terry heard the sharp intake of breath. That had shut her up. Yet now of course, he felt sorry.

She spoke first.

"I just wanted to tell you that there's another screening tonight. I know you've had one already, but I think we're in far more trouble than they'll admit to," she said, "It's in Meta York, Hospice twenty-seven, fifteen-thirty hours. Please, please come."

"*I've been trying to!*"

That particular one escaped almost involuntarily.

"Of course you have," she said, her scepticism heavy in her voice, "It must be a hard reputation to live up to."

He had thoroughly deserved that, and he knew it.

"Why isn't this *out*?" he wanted to know.

"You know full well why," his mother's voice echoed within his cranium, "The choice is either take it or don't, but you cannot bring any others. If you do, as I said, the entire facility will be relocated and the present one destroyed. This is *underground*, do you understand? There just aren't enough facilities."

Terry looked at Kim. This sweet, young thing was a few years younger than him. She wouldn't understand - there'd be friends, family and their friends whom she'd want to save in addition to herself. Did he really want to risk his entire life for this simple, easy, pleasant moment? There would be others, and she wouldn't even know what he'd done before it was too late to say anything.

She was sweet.

But many girls of her age were sweet. A few years would flesh out both their bones and their tongues. Did he need it?

Play false. It was like his mum said; Kim didn't even need to know.

"Yeah," he whispered with a slight grin, "That makes perfect sense."

The line went dead.

"Was that important?" Kim asked him.

He looked into her innocent, playful, green eyes and he smiled.

"Nah," he said, "Mum's just being pedantic again. Now,

where were we?"

Kim gasped in delight as Terry took a firm hold of her and resumed his affections.

It was nearly ten past eight when Kim sat up in happy fatigue, reached past her sated lover and turned on the TVNet.

The scores of music channels she flipped quickly through were playing the most banal video-pap, from 'Don't Need No Midgets In My Porno', by the Virgin Mothers, to 'Purity Of My Skin', by the Slut Fetish Whore Dogs Of Sodom. It was something of a relief to find the nearest news channel.

And here was Terry's dad, preaching his just and terrible vengeance upon the terrorists. Kim looked at Terry for a judgement.

"Oh, go on then," he said, "Let's hear what the old sod has to say."

She turned up the sound a little.

"And we shall not rest," Bleoche was sternly announcing, "We shall not falter, we shall not stumble, we shall return tenfold upon our enemy the injuries and injustices which he has..."

The look of abject horror and confusion in President Antoine Bleoche's eyes, as the blood gushed out of him from every orifice, was quickly overcome as his eyes too became awash with crimson and he dropped down dead to the floor, out of the camera's field of vision.

Terry squawked in shock. He sat stunned, unable to move his eyes from the screen. The screen shot itself didn't change either, and this began to trouble him even more. They'd have cut to black, surely? But what am I thinking, he wondered absently, I've just seen...

Why was his hand wet? The pounding horror rushed up his spine and into his brain, and without even turning around to see her, he wretched. The warm, sticky liquid was all down his legs too, and under his naked behind.

Terry screamed and leapt from the bed. Kim lay upon the large, slowly-spreading, deep red stain, staring vacantly upwards. Those gorgeous breasts which he had nuzzled fervently, less than half an hour ago, her tousled hair, that love-bite upon her neck, the eyes - draining blood slowly...

He screamed again, in anger, in pain, in dread; in emotions he had never had to even acknowledge before.

He had been with her all night, and it was contagious. He had to get another screening, and fast. For the first time since he could remember, Terry Bleoche found himself in a mortal panic, and wanting his mummy. He had to get out.

In the maddened rush to pull on his clothes, he caught sight of himself in the mirror. The view showed more of his father in his face than he had ever seen before.

The tears were coming now, thick and fast and uncontrollable. He bawled in helpless anguish, and broke the mirror with his fist.

- adapted from 'OUT OF PHASE', © H. R. Brown;
Book III of 'The PHASE Trilogy'.
26/06/2002

THE RIDE

Joe couldn't feel anything. It had been that way since Charlie had gone. The cell next to his was now occupied by a giant, sombre man who seemed to be practically mute. Joe had tried to speak to him many times, to complain about the food, to ask him random questions about his life, or merely to try to at least gain his name.

Occasionally Joe would find himself granted a grunt, in reply. He couldn't even see his new neighbour from behind the bars which ran across the entrances to all the cells, and his was the last on the Row.

The Row. He felt almost well disposed to it now, now they had finally come for him. Even in spite of all the interminable silences of the last few months since the departure of his friend Charlie, he now looked back upon his time here with a sorrow whose gentle nature he could not have imagined when he was first put in.

Even in silence, the mind may wander over valleys and mountains lit by warm sunsets, it may raise a family spanning multiple generations; it may rise and fall in spirit with the same senses of passion, anger, delight, sorrow and laughter as those who live in warmth and companionship - when one has good books to read.

Now that his time had come upon him, Joe knew not what to think. He had long dreaded the slow frying of the electrical current, through his entire body. He had tortured himself with thoughts of the eventual gratefulness he would find in his own demise, when all pain and life was fading from him, the delicious sense of *release* -

Yet, to what?

What did he really believe?

As the guards and the Reverend were entering his cell and reading him the script in thick, southern, military tones, Joe found himself thinking again of the things Charlie had said to him on his final night here. His words had had a profound effect upon Joe. He had thought of them every hour of every day since.

That night had seemed eternal. The pair had not mentioned that there would be no sleep tonight, but it was understood. What man could sleep knowing the dawn would be his end?

The night may be awful dark,

And sunlight no respite,

Yet what's to burn and spark,

But to open and see the light?"

Or so it ran in a little couplet which a previous occupant had once carved lovingly into the wall of Joe's cell, just above the head of his bunk. The words had been there for five years and Joe had long since forgotten about them, until that night. That night he had read them to Charlie for the first time ever. The words had become something almost religious in Joe's mind and he had to share the thought with his friend, if only that it offered him hope when his death was at hand.

Charlie had opened his mouth and roared with fiendish laughter.

"No way man?! It *says* that!"

"Yeah, man. I s'pose it's pretty funny!"

"No, no!" said Charlie, "It's a part of... well, you know."

Joe became puzzled.

"No," he said, "What are you on about?"

Now Charlie was puzzled.

"You've been here how long?" he said, "And you're saying you don't know about the Reminders?!"

"Reminders of what?"

"Jesus!" said Charlie, "You're probably up soon after me - *and no-one's told you*!?!"

"Told me what?"

"Oh my God! Kid, you've gotta be kiddin' me. You've been here five years! Five years and no-one's told you! That's gotta be a record!"

Joe was growing impatient. "Told me *what*?" he demanded.

In the very here and now, Joe was being handcuffed, ready

for the final departure from his cell. They pulled him up onto his feet and gathered his arms behind his back, where his wrists were fastened together with the dismal efficiency of cold steel. In his head, the advent calendar was still playing out, on one level. He had seen this last stretch like a series of apocalyptic milestones, each one closer to that miracle morning than the last - and now they were coming thick and fast. He was being taken out of the cell, but inwardly he was reliving the conversation's he had had with Charlie on that fateful night, once more:

Charlie had reached his arm out of his cell and round the corner, that he might grasp the hand of his brother-in-waiting. Joe took it and gripped it firmly, and Charlie began to spill the secret.

Before Joe had a chance to think on those words again, he had a monumental surprise. As the guards led him out of his dull, grey cell and into the grim, ashen corridor, past his neighbour, that big, quiet man stepped quickly up to the bars, reached out his hands and grasped hold of Joe's arm.

"Let me speak to him!" the big man implored the guards who were now trying to separate the two of them.

The guards looked at Joe, who couldn't hide his surprise.

"Let him speak," said Joe, "Please, let me hear him."

The guards shrugged and waited.

The big man gave Joe a little smile. "Sorry I've been quiet," he said, "But I want you to know that it won't be long now. Your brothers are waiting for you."

Now it was Joe's turn to grunt at his neighbour. "What, in heaven?!" he scoffed.

"No man," said the giant, "At the gates of the next Ride!"

Joe felt something not unlike hope itself, flickering through his deadened mind. The giant had just given him a Reminder; a gift in itself so great that Charlie's final words to him, so often thought of with dreadful pessimism, now seemed to offer something he had never dared to hope for.

The guards carried him - sagging slightly as he was with the sublime epiphany now flowering in his brain - down the corridor towards his date with fate.

Now, he heard old Charlie's words once again;

"There is no need to worry," Charlie had told him, "The Day will be the end of this life, *but it most definitely is not the end.*"

Joe had realised he must be patient with his friend. He was obviously reaching the edges of sanity, in his nearness to death. Sad, really. Horrifying, to imagine that he could end up going through a similar process, when his end came -

He was being taken down the corridor towards a big, iron door, but he was being taken by silent guards with their heads down; he was trapped in the vicelike jaws of the soulless machine which was going to put an end to his existence.

A bluebottle buzzed past his head, and Joe thought, 'Hey, wait for it!' Suddenly the guards were shocked as he broke out into loud chuckles. They looked at each other, worried and uneasy.

And, in his unwillingness to face the finality of his own death, Joe was speaking once more to his good friend Charlie, on that fateful night -

"Look mate, I know this is kind of imminent in your eyes, and I'm sorry to have to say it, but if getting fried alive until we be dead is not the end - what the hell *is*? I don't know of any heaven I can believe in, and you're not telling me you're suddenly a born-again Christian!?"

Charlie had laughed. "You really haven't been told, have you? You know, I'd heard they were looking trying to keep a lid on it - to do it to people who didn't know, just to see how lost they'd be. I'm amazed you don't know about it already - you've been here for five years!"

"What the hell you talking about!?" Joe had yelled at him.

"This life is just a Ride, man. You'll see it too, when it's your turn. Your friends will be waiting for you and it'll all come back. The human race, my friend, is collection of inter-dimensional surfers, party people and head cases, and we're all at an infinite, cosmic, pan-dimensional fair, or festival, if you like. We're near the end of this Ride, is all. There'll be plenty more!"

Joe had been silent for a while. They'd never really had a theological discussion before, and finally being allowed a glimpse of Charlie's belief system was somewhat startling. It was a bit of a crazy one, but hell, if it was what kept his friend going he wasn't going to knock it now, with the Hour falling so soon upon Charlie's head.

In the end, Joe had chuckled. "That's cool man! Always the optimist, and now I know why!"

"It's no trick man," Charlie had assured him, "You'll see, when you're up! OK, so we messed up this ride, treated it like a game to be won, not like a ride to be enjoyed - and so they're burning us out of it. It's all cool; we can all go again, no problem!"

"I tell you what," said Joe, "If this is true - I'm innocent! That means I can get my money back!"

"Still with the innocent line, huh?"

"OK smart ass - you check it out with the ticket master when you get to this 'cosmic fair' you've been telling me about, in two hours from now. You'll see!"

"You know what, man?" Charlie had said, laughing, "I'm gonna do that!"

And now, finally, Joe was here. The guards had brought him his stomach-clenching first view of The Chair. *His* Chair. This was it. Just a Ride, he told himself, just a Ride at the cosmic fair. The giant in the cell next to his had given him what he needed to dare to believe in it...

He was strapped in. A mask was pulled down over his face. A damp sponge was placed on his head, before the cap was brought down. The Reverend read him the last rights and asked him to repent.

The blue bottle was still buzzing around somewhere nearby, and the crazed part of his mind said, 'Go on, land on my cap!'

Why these stupid thoughts?! He wondered, ... *'don't worry man, it's just a* ride'..

Yet he restrained himself from laughing. This was his last chance to speak his mind.

"I didn't kill that woman," he said, quietly, "It is all of you who should repent for what you are about to do."

There was a touch of impatient inexperience about the guard whose job it was to throw the switch. Hearing this blasphemy from the condemned man, he looked quickly around at his superiors, questioning them in silent urgency.

Captain Pear was a man who had seen more of these than he could count, he was already bored and so he gave a quick nod to the excited youngster at the switch.

Joe was instantly stricken with the bolts of Zeus, back arching, blistering pain coursing through his entire body. He couldn't scream, he could only fry and burn. In the midst of his agony, with the turmoil of his boiling blood writhing within him, his mind began to collapse as it sensed the end at hand, and that this ghastly surrender was inevitable, that it really would be a *release...*

Through the haze, he thought he could hear lively shouts and wild colours were starting to rush everywhere, calling him, carrying him into the rainbow. "Where the hell have you been!" someone cried, "Here he is!" said another, "He's back!" and then he saw Charlie come running towards him, shouting

"Hey, Joe man! You win! Innocent after all, huh? Sorry I doubted you man. You memories'll be messed up for while, you might not know it right now, but there's no money to claim back for your Ride - this is the Infinite Fair man, we don't need money, not now, not *ever*! Do you wanna go again?"

dedicated to the memory of the late prophet;
Bill Hicks

© H R Brown, 28/09/2003

ABOUT THE AUTHOR

Born: Leeds, 1977
Education: BSc Hons III; Mathematics, University of
Manchester, 1999

H. R. Brown is either a gestalt entity or a functioning
schizophrenic, depending on your viewpoint. The main
constituent characters which comprise this man are; Poet,
Pirate, Logician, Cynic and Horny Toad, but by no means in
that order.

He has worked variously as a farm hand, non-paid teaching
assistant, car valet, warehouse hand helping sell farm
supplies, floor mopper in the oven section of a tumble-dryer
factory, box factory shipping assistant, fibre-glass packer
and binman. He has also done shifts crewing for the Royal
Exchange Theatre in Manchester, there was one paid strip-
act and he sang in a couple of ill-fated rock bands. Since the
turn of the century he has done mostly office work, as well
as one paid day as an official minibus driver.

Printed in Great Britain
by Amazon

72356382R00149